CHASING SHADOWS

By
D. J. McAllister

ISBN: 978-0-692-59291-5

Design: Dedicated Book Services, (www.netdbs.com)

DEDICATION

To all the Military Members, Veterans, First Responders, and Emergency Personnel who save our lives and protect the American People on a daily basis.

Many thanks to Betty, who without her, these books would not have been completed.

If you liked this book please post a photo of this cover on your Facebook account or other media so your friends will know where to buy this book.

AMAZON.COM / Books / djmcallister

TABLE OF CONTENTS

FOREWORD

Sometimes we sit around the house or the places where we meet our friends and complain about the government and taxes and anything else we can think of to complain about. Most of us aren't old enough to remember Hitler and his fixation with the Jews and his twisted beliefs that the Jews caused all of Germany's troubles.

Sometimes I sit and think, What if?

What if Hitler's fixation was with English speaking people. It seems to me that these people would have been easier to find in Germany speaking German with a English accent than German speaking Jews.

What if Hitler had been born in England or The United States of America? Would the people of these countries have listened to his demented rantings? You don't think so? Well maybe not in the 1930's, but what about a century later.

What if the "Hitler" figure was born and raised in the United States. What if he really looked and talked like a nice guy, he didn't beat his fists and scream like a madman.

What if he made a good sounding series of points that told the citizens that their troubles of the age were attributed to a particular race or group of people living in the United States?

Of course our immediate response is to say, "No, not me!"

But with the proper brain washing and finger pointing you might be one who would agree to the total extermination of one "Terrible" race of people.

This is the story of three people, their loves and hates, their hopes and fears and our hope for the future. Our story begins in January of the new millennium and proceeds forty three years through some very dark times.

Hitler believed that the reality of Germany would improve if the Jews were eliminated. But there are many realities. One man's reality is another's fantasy and it is fantasy to think that the human species can ever live without fear, hate, crime, envy or jealousy.

Read on. Read on.

Chapter 1

Entering The 21st Century

January 2000

The mood of the world at the beginning of the twenty-first century was a continuation of the turmoil and tensions which existed during the end of the nineteen nineties. There were racial tensions in every city in the United States as well as cities around the world.

There was finger pointing in all directions, especially by politicians and the media, and mostly at each other. The rights of the citizens continued to dwindle, not just those of the so-called minorities, but life in general continued to be eroded at every turn by the Federal Government.

Increasing crime, drugs, youth pregnancies, the continuing lack of jobs for the young and old, and rights of every ethnic group were slowly being taken away by that same Federal Government of the people and for the people.

Whenever possible, lands and personal property of minorities were also confiscated by the government through one of its many money conscious agencies. The term "minorities" has been recently expanded by President Henderson to include all people who are unlike or disliked by the government.

1

During January of the year 2000, there were three children born who would change the world. These three children were born in Valley Lutheran Hospital located in the town they would call home for many years to come, and though none of these three would know until much later, their lives were intertwined with one another from the beginning.

Casey MacKenzie was the first born and the only son of Ann and Michael MacKenzie, both of Scottish families. Teresa Basilio, a daughter of Marie and Tony Basilio, Marie is half Cherokee and Tony is Italian. Mitchell Cordell, the son, and only child of Inga and Herschell Cordell, Inga is Swedish and Herschell is German.

Mitchell was one of the very few blonde haired children living in the area. Most are like Teresa, a mixture of one or more of the American Indian tribes, Mexican or other Spanish speaking races. Or they might be like Casey, a dark haired European child. From the first, little Mitchell was a real curiosity for the other kids his age.

All three lived on Skyline Street in a little town just east of Mesa, Arizona called Apache Junction. The MacKenzies lived next door to the Basilios and across the street was the Cordell's house.

The back yards of Casey and Teresa led straight out to a field and on up into the mountains. There's not many trees in this part of the country, but Apache Junction backs up to the Superstition Mountains where the paloverde and the mesquite trees grow quite large along with the saguaro and the jumping cholla cactus.

Nobody who lives in this part of the country tries to fool themselves about the weather or the climate around here. There are only three seasons in the Phoenix area, early summer, summer and late summer. In short, it's hot and dry all the time.

"Today is May 19 2002. Good evening. In world news tonight, an earthquake registering five point one on the Richter scale shook the southern mountains of Chile last night. Had it not been for a few peasants living in the area, no one in the local area would have known about it." The television announcer said.

Mitchell's dad has always liked to watch the news on CNN and the Congressional Channel and tried to keep up on all the events of the day, no matter how insignificant.

The beginning of the twenty first century was also exciting for many astronomers, when late in the fall of 2002, one of them found a brand new comet. The first astronomer to see and report the new celestial being was Dr. William R. Ashford.

Previously an unknown in the field, but after this amazing discovery, became world famous. Unfortunately that fame was short lived when other scientists and astronomers discovered that Ashford's Comet was traveling a course which would bring it dangerously close to the earth.

For months after the initial discovery by Ashford, all eyes of the scientific world were focused on the comet. Tales of death and destruction were printed in every newspaper, magazine and tabloid in every country of the world and they all blamed William Ashford. A headline in one of the supermarket tabloids read, "Ashford's Comet Will Kill Millions!"

Talk shows abounded with "learned" scientists getting their names on television and their hands into the till. However, not one of the so-called experts knew any more about the comet and it's eventual path than the general public who these greedy opportunists were trying to influence.

No two of these so-called geniuses could agree even on the size of this mysterious body or the distance this new unnamed comet would pass by the earth. Some said it would crash into the earth and others gave a variety of scientific sounding alternatives.

"Tonight on The Late Show with David Letterman, the noted scientist who discovered the comet that is right now hurtling toward earth, Dr. William Ashford. And now, here's David Letterman." Dave did his monologue and right after the commercial break, introduced Dr. Ashford.

"It's nice to meet you Dr. Ashford. It says here that you have a Ph.D. in Astronomy. I guess that means that you're an expert." Dave said.

"It is true that I have studied astronomy and that I know a little about it." He said.

"Would you answer some very important questions for us? First, how big is this comet that you discovered?"

"It is about the size of Rhode Island, only round, about thirty miles across. That means it is about thirty thousand cubic miles of mass." He said.

The people in the audience all made a shocked noise and a hush came over the whole studio.

"Wow! It's a big one!" Dave said with a stunned look on his face. "What is it made of?"

"Mostly ice and rock and various unknown materials."

"Why unknown?" Dave asked.

"Because there are many materials in this vast universe that we have never encountered, and this little bit of rock we are calling a comet is still many millions of miles away."

"When will it be here?" Dave asked.

"I would say it will be within a week or so."

"Is it going to hit the earth?"

"I don't think so."

"That's not the exact words we wanted to hear from you. Don't you have a better answer?" Dave said.

Dave reached down into a drawer and pulled out a brightly colored red, yellow and white tabloid with the headline reading, "Ashford's Comet Will Kill Millions." "What do you think of this, Doc?" Dave asked.

"That reporter hasn't got a clue. Actually there are five different scenarios. May I use your blackboard? I seem to be able to talk better when I'm standing at a board." The audience politely chuckled. It was the first sound which came from the audience since Dr. Ashford shocked them initially.

Dr. Ashford stood and walked to the white board which had been previously placed there and took one of the colored marking pens.

"Scenario number one, the comet will hit another body and not come anywhere close to earth. It might run into Jupiter or some other celestial body and therefore, not continue on it's present course."

Dr. Ashford drew circles and lines to illustrate his scenario for the studio audience and the cameras which panned around the stage.

"Number two, it will continue on its present path and not come near earth. This is quite possible, these bodies do not make a habit of running into each other in space."

Dr. Ashford hurriedly erased and redrew his illustration for the new point which he explained.

"Number three, it will hit earth with a glancing blow and continue on. Let's skip this one for now."

The silence in the studio grew deeper with each word he spoke. After that last remark, you could have heard a pin drop.

"There are two parts to number four. Part one, it will hit a large land mass, and part two, it will hit a large body of water on the earth."

Dave is trying his best to smile, but that last one wiped the smile right off his face.

"You're a bundle of laughs tonight, Doc. You said earlier that the reporter hasn't got a clue, what did you mean by that?"

"Very simply, if a comet this size would hit the earth at the speed we know it to be traveling, say in the middle of Kansas, or Brazil, or Siberia, it would make a crater large enough that the dust and other material thrown up into the air by the force of the impact, would obliterate the sun for more than a year and every living thing on earth would die."

Dr. Ashford paused to catch his breath and the silence in the studio was deafening. He spoke again almost in a whisper.

"As I said, that reporter doesn't have a clue."

"What about part two of that last one?" Dave asked.

"Same result." Dr. Ashford said matter-of-factly.

The silence was so thick you could cut it with a knife. Dave's face turned ashen and it was amazing how good Dave looked right then for a man of his age. Dr. Ashford began again.

"The problem with these journalists, and especially these tabloid writers is this. Not one of them have had the training necessary to make the kinds of statements that they so often make. Do you know what they went to school for?"

"Journalism?" Dave said.

"Yes, of course! Journalism!" He spat the word out like he was spitting out a bug. "Not astronomy, physics, engineering or any other technical discipline, but they have the gall to write garbage like this!" Having finished, Dr. Ashford threw the paper on the floor. It skittered across the waxed floor and out into the audience.

"You certainly get fired up, don't you Doc?" Dave said trying for all he was worth to smile.

"Yes, I'm sorry. Now let me explain what I think will actually happen."

"I hope this story is better than your last one, my heart might not take another one like that." Dave said. "You scared me a little." Dave's face was still ashen and pasty colored.

Dr. Ashford went back to the board and began to draw a large circle around a smaller circle in the center labeled "Sun" on the board.

"This is the path of the earth around the sun. This is the projected path of the comet." He said drawing a straight line intersecting the circle.

"I think the comet will pass very close to us in a few days and the earth will pass through its tail allowing cosmic dust to fall to earth. This then, will be a good chance for more, possibly amazing, discoveries by collecting the dust and analyzing the particles found therein very carefully."

Dr. Ashford concluded his remarks and returned to his seat. Dave jumped up and tried to get the audience to applaud, but the feeling of helplessness pervaded the studio and I'm sure, the whole country, that precious few hand claps were heard.

When the day finally arrived, Ashford's Comet made it's closest pass at the earth on March 17, 2003, when the earth passed through the comet's tail, just as Dr. Ashford had predicted several days before. The earth was bathed in dust and particles for a period of only two minutes and eighteen seconds as the two bodies moved together in space.

Scientists from every country in the world were conducting experiments of every sort during that time. Collecting and recording data from previously unknown radiation and particles that were collected from sites all around the world.

Teresa didn't have much to say to her mother that day. The little girl was echoing those words being spoken by many other children of the area that day.

"Mommy, I don't feel good." Teresa whined.

"I'm trying honey, I'm trying." Her mother said. "I'm going to take you to the doctor."

Maria Basilio and Teresa were entering Dr. Jennings' office for their ten a.m. appointment.

"Hi, Maria." The voice said from the other side of the room. Maria and Teresa both looked over to see Ann MacKenzie with Casey looking very sick and forlorn.

"Hi, Ann, Casey has it too, I see."

"Hi, Teresa." Casey moaned.

"Hi, Casey." Teresa moaned back.

The receptionist stepped into the room, "Mrs. MacKenzie, you can take Casey back now."

They were back in only a few minutes.

"What did the doctor say?" Maria asked.

He said it's the same thing that all the kids have, he gave me a prescription and said to keep him in bed for four or five days." Ann replied.

"Maybe we won't have to worry about it if the comet crashes into the earth tonight."

"Don't talk like that!"

Casey and Teresa were in bed sick during that day and for five days after the comet's visit, the two three year olds caught a case of the flu and they weren't letting go.

Both of the two kids were too sick to go to their window and look out as the comet passed by that night, but it looked like the moon was passing the earth in the night sky wearing a long shiny tail.

Scientists rushed to publish their findings, but just as those who talked doom and gloom only a few days prior to it's arrival, those new findings were equally unresolved and worthless.

Each and every scientific paper that was published differed from every other paper. None could agree on even one single little point. It will take much time and several dedicated intelligent scientific detectives to determine the consequences of the comet's visit to earth.

It wasn't long before strange things began to occur all around the world and little by little almost without notice, the complexion of the earth and its peoples were affected.

Environmental problems were becoming more and more serious every day. Air, water and land were found more polluted and less of these important resources are available to us each year. But, people, a renewable resource, began to show the most outrageous changes of all.

People were becoming more furious toward each other and even toward animals and inanimate objects. "Road Rage", a term coined ten years earlier, had become an almost uncontrollable fad among drivers of all ages during the year 2004.

Most drivers were carrying guns of all sizes, shapes and descriptions and at the slightest provocation, were shooting other drivers, passengers and pedestrians for no apparent reason.

Of course, nothing would be done by the Federal Government until one or two of their own were directly affected, and on one bright summer day in 2005, during the Congressional break and within hours of each other, the senior Senator from New York and a Congressman from Michigan were killed by enraged motorists.

The morning of the Monday after Labor Day, September 8th, 2005 began in the US Senate with Vice President Ericsson speaking.

"The Senate will come to order. The chair recognizes the esteemed Senator from Illinois. Senator Cooke you have the floor."

Senator Cooke rose to his feet and walked quickly to the microphone.

"I bring to you this morning a long standing and debilitating problem that we here in the Congress of the United States must quickly deal with. That problem is called by many, Road Rage. I call it murder!" He said.

"In a study from 1990 to 1996 on the road rage phenomenon, ten thousand and thirty seven incidents of road rage were found and examined. There were two hundred eighteen men, women and children killed, and twelve thousand eight hundred and ten innocent people injured.

Of these ten thousand and thirty seven incidents, forty four hundred of them involved weapons of one sort or another. These weapons include clubs, fists, feet, firearms and knives. In twelve hundred and fifty of these incidents, the weapon used was larger than these I have just listed.

You ask, what weapon could be larger than these. An automobile is larger than these. An automobile is larger and can certainly be used as a weapon. These enraged motorists tried and sometimes, many times, succeeded in running their victims down with their car."

"Further, in a study from 1996 to 2002, the numbers rose markedly to sixty five thousand two hundred forty incidents of road rage during the period under study. There were fourteen hundred seventeen people killed, and eighty one thousand nine hundred sixty five people injured. There were twenty eight thousand six hundred incidents involving weapons, and eighty one hundred and twenty five run down with a car."

"Appalling? Yes! It is hard for me to stand here before you today and recite these statistics to you without feeling some rage myself."

"Further, in a continuing study from 2002 to the present, completed only recently, more people, more men, women and children were killed this year from road rage than from automobile accidents in the last ten years. There were one million eight hundred twenty six thousand seven hundred twenty incidents.

Let me say that again. There were one million eight hundred twenty six thousand seven hundred and twenty incidents of uncontrolled rage which have ended in violence."

"My fellow members of the Senate, we must stop this senseless maiming and murdering of the innocent people of our nation here and now. Let me continue! There were, during these last two years, thirty nine thousand six hundred seventy six people killed last year alone, and one million two hundred ninety five thousand and twenty men, women and children injured by these roving marauders driving their cars and killing our citizens. There were eight hundred thousand eight hundred incidents involving weapons, and two hundred twenty thousand five hundred of them involving the perpetrator's automobile in a hit and run situation."

"Eighty percent of the time, when a weapon is drawn in these kind of occasions, it is used. Eighty percent! That is outrageous!"

"And only last month, while we were all visiting with our constituents during the Congressional work break, the esteemed Senator Mahan from New York, and Congressman Benson from Michigan, who many of us knew and respected, were killed on the same day by the kind of hoodlums that I am here speaking to you about."

"I would like to read from this bill I hold in my hand, which Congressman Smith and I are cosponsoring to eliminate the carnage which is going on out there in the streets."

Senator Cooke read through the bill and there was an immediate call for a vote on the bill. The vote passed with only twenty-three dissenting votes. The bill was then hand carried to the House and to the bill's co-sponsor, Congressman Samuel Smith.

Just after lunch, Congressman Smith addressed the House with much the same words as were spoken earlier in the Senate that morning by Senator Cooke. And as it had been in the Senate previously, a call for the vote was issued and the bill passed by an even wider margin in the lower house.

Shortly after the bill passed the House vote, this wonderful crime stopping bill was again hand carried, this time to the Office of the President, who signed it at five p.m. sharp, Washington local time, just in time for the television cameras to record the event for the evening news, taking in all the drama of the moment and recording for the public, this great political victory of the President of the United States.

"Good evening. In national news tonight an item from the nation's capital. In response to the growing phenomena, the Federal Government enacted emergency legislation empowering all police from those at the Federal level and State Highway Patrol to the local small town cop, to shoot and kill the offender at the scene, if it could be proven through eye-witness testimony that the offender was exhibiting Road Rage against other innocent victims."

"If the offender was taken into custody after a drive-by shooting and through a trial, proven to have killed while under the influence of "Road Rage", he is to be executed without appeal after the completion of a calendar week from the end of the trial."

More than fifty percent of the offenders caught during the first year were executed on the highways and streets of the nation. The legislation also required that most of these were to be cremated to save space in cemeteries around the country. Another twenty four percent of the original number were given a trial and executed shortly thereafter.

Road Rage was down by more than fifty percent by the end of 2006. Of course, when nearly a million and a half people are killed on response to the growing road rage fad, people took notice. However, it didn't appear that the road rage phenomena would go away soon. Some outside force seemed to be driving it.

Our three young people growing up in the southwest have started first grade this year at Superstition Mountain Elementary School and Teresa and Casey were very excited about it. Teresa and Casey have played together since they were born and both were excited about starting school. Neither had met Mitchell before that first day of school. Mister Cordel didn't want his son contaminated by black-haired heathens.

One day early in the school year the teacher, Mrs. Putnam, posed a question to each of her first grade students.

"When you grow up, what do you want to be?" Asked Mrs. Putnam of the class.

A simple question designed to make them begin to think for themselves and bring out the shy student.

"Manuel, we'll start with you. When you grow up, what do you want to be?"

"I want to be a doctor like on TV."

"Teresa, you're next."

"I want to feed the world."

"Maria."

"I want to be a nurse."

"Casey."

"I want to save the world."

"Benjamin."

"I want to be a baker like my father."

"Mitchell."

"I want to be King of the World."

"You? You're a little boy from a backwater town no one ever heard of, how can you be the king of the world? Your hair isn't even the right color. No one has yellow hair." The girl next to him said and laughed at him.

Then all the kids laughed at him and Mitchell's face got very red and he got very mad. She was right though, no one in that school besides Mitchell had yellow hair.

"I'll get you for this." He screamed as he ran out of the room.

When Mitchell told his father about how the kids laughed at him and made fun of him, his father told him that most of the kids in the Phoenix area are Indian, Mexican and half-breeds, his father's name for them, and they all got special privileges that real Americans like Mitchell don't get.

"Don't worry son, someday you will have the last laugh." Mitchell's dad said.

Soon the story was getting around the school and all the kids in the other grades were laughing at him. Mitchell vowed then and there to get them all for the embarrassment and humiliation they had put him through, and the die was cast.

Casey and Mitchell went all through elementary school together, in the same classes and Mitchell was a bully even then. Casey was his favorite target, even though he was not Indian or Spanish speaking, he had dark hair like them and that was good enough for him. But Mitchell enjoyed spreading it around to any kid who might be unlucky enough to be in the way of his unbalanced, bigoted feelings.

Most bigots are a little unbalanced anyway and Mitchell is definitely taking after his father in that regard, who has taught him everything he knows. Dad doesn't like anyone who isn't of European decent and then none of those Mediterranean types. Too bad there isn't a vaccination for prejudice.

Strangely enough, even though Mitchell was bigger than most of the kids in his class, and he acted so stupid sometimes, he was smart and learned everything in school very quickly. School came very easy for him. He never needed to take any of his books home since he finished all of his assigned homework during classes. Therefore, the teachers all liked him, but because of his bullying tactics, all the kids didn't.

Casey, on the other hand, always had to scratch for every ounce of knowledge he ever acquired. He studied during school, carried his books and homework home every day and worked long past dark to complete it.

Fortunately, once he finally got it, it was locked into his brain forever, but it always seemed to take a little more for the information to penetrate his consciousness. And of course, Mitchell would fight with

Casey on the way home from school every day. Casey was an easier target when he was carrying books and Mitchell always liked to pick the easier targets for his cruelty.

Chapter 2
Chɑrlɘs III

June 2007

June in Belgium and Holland is a beautiful time of year. There are flowers blooming everywhere and trees and bushes of lush green covering the landscape. The trees, bushes and flowers all blend together with the houses and farms of the area to form a beautiful tableau of peace and harmony.

An obsession, even a fanaticism with things that are "mine" began slowly in every country and region of the world and grew slowly to phenomenal proportions. In June of 2007, a fight, not a war, began between two normally peaceable men, who even though they did not know one another, and did not have any obvious quarrel with the other, began to fight with each other. For some reason, unknown to either of the men, they felt an uncontrollable urge to fight. So they did.

Other men in the vicinity of the first two men joined into the fight, because they too, felt an urge to fight. Before the day was out, there were hundreds of men along the border of Holland and Belgium in towns like Knokke, Maldegem and Terneuzen fighting with each other.

These men were not fighting as Dutch against Belgians, it was just men fighting with men. There were men in the cities and towns, in the hills and the fields. There were millers and tinkers, and cobblers and tailors, haberdashers and milliners, clothiers and accouters. There were factory workers and welders, mechanics and store owners, farmers and truck drivers.

Once, a group of women joined the fray, but because of the greater strength of the men, the women were whipped soundly soon after they began. Four of the wives of the men who the women had begun to fight jumped into the melee, and all the women standing around observing this spectacle joined into their own separate "female" fight.

Soon the fight, a typical old time fist fight, raged along the border of the two countries until men and women from all around the countryside came to join in the fight. It wore on for weeks until nearly every person from both countries was involved in the fight in one way or another. Women and children helped carry food and water and bandages for the injured, the more seriously injured were carried away to medical facilities for help.

It spread to other towns along the border as well. Little towns like Bergen op Zoom, Kalmthout and Zundert, Wuustwezel, Turnhout and Weldhoven. By the end of the eighth week, the fight had spread all the way to Weert and Maaseik.

Television stations feed on this kind of thing like mosquitoes feed on a sweaty man and shortly after the news of the fight reached one of the larger cities in Europe and was fed around the world, crews began to show up with their cameras and microphones.

Soon photographers from England, France and the United States appeared with blood thirsty looks on their faces and cameras in their hands, poised at the ready. All of these insipid snap shooters were sent off as fast as their shutters could click with their tail between their legs after being thrashed soundly by one or more of the people they came to observe and interview.

Most news reports around the world talked of the "demented" and "deranged" behavior of the participants in this first ever international fist fight. It has become an established criteria that the media must label everything in order to make it fit their time slotted sound bites, and their name for this event was "The Big Fight".

Many of the media people ridiculed the "unbalanced", as they put it, men and women of Belgium and Holland who were taking part in this ridiculous obsession. Isn't it amazing how many reporters can write stories and reports about what they have neither any idea, nor facts to base their comments.

It soon became a game between the participating Dutch and Belgians to see who could beat up a paparazzi and destroy his camera the fastest. Each time, during one of these little games, the fighting would stop so all the people could watch and cheer as another camera carrier was pummeled into the ground by a neighbor or a former adversary.

After fourteen weeks of fighting, with people lying on the ground who were totally exhausted, for miles and miles along the border, two men stood and shook hands and it was over. A TV reporter perched in front of his camera there in the middle of the meadow shoved a microphone, and the TV camera his sidekick was carrying, into the face of the last two men standing and asked, "Do you like fighting?"

Whereupon both men turned and looked at each other and smiled, then punched both the cameraman and the reporter in the face and yelled, "Yes!" Thereby ending the interview, and leaving the ambitious, inquiring journalists lying face down on the ground and all the men within earshot of the "interview" standing around them laughing and cheering.

Later, days after everyone had gone home and cooled off, when questioned by reporters, television interviewers and camera personalities, not one man could say why he felt the willingness, even eagerness, to enter into the fight. On the evening news, the one question that all the television news personalities asked, but left unanswered was, "What do you suppose caused this?"

In second grade Mitchell was continuing to beat up Casey on a daily basis and had begun to fight with everyone else in the class, including the girls. One day on the way to school, Mitchell grabbed Casey's homework and tore it up in front of everyone in the school yard and laughed and beat his chest saying how big and strong and terrific he was. Teresa and some of her other girl friends consoled Casey as Mitchell strode proudly into the school ready to begin the day.

Later during second period when the teacher called for the homework to be turned in, Casey carried his homework up to the teacher and handed it to her himself.

"Thank you, Casey."

Mitchell jumped up and said, "Wait! I tore that up already! Everybody saw me tear it up! You can't hand that in!"

Mitchell then swung a fist at Casey, but missed since be was too far from him. The teacher, Mrs. Ramirez, promptly took Mitchell to the principal's office, with Mitchell yelling back at Casey, "I'll get you for this." Mitchell has told Casey that he would get him for one thing or another from the beginning of first grade.

Casey began making two copies of his homework some time ago for just an occasion as this. It looks like there may be some hope for the not-so-bright Casey after all.

Mrs. Ramirez second grade class were just beginning the training to use the Virtual Classroom, it can take you any place in time, real or imagined, where the children in the class may experience the actual historical event with the aid of the helmet inside the bubble. The teacher has been introducing it to them one class at a time and the first class would be History.

"Alright, everyone to your seats. The date is November 19, 1863 and we are seated in the audience in the middle of a field where a great battle was recently fought and Edward Everett has just completed one of his greatest speeches he had ever given. He spoke for two full hours, and now we see a tall thin man wearing a stovepipe hat stand and approach the crowd. Listen." Mrs. Ramirez said.

The class was transfixed as the tall lanky man spoke.

"Four score and seven years ago our fathers brought forth on this continent, a new nation, conceived in Liberty, and dedicated to the proposition that all men are created equal."

Casey studied the tall thin man as he spoke. His words seemed to pierce his very soul. This man, this Lincoln, was speaking directly to him. Casey was no more than a few feet from him, looking up at him. It was almost as if Casey could touch him, and Lincoln had touched Casey. How could a man who died a hundred and fifty years ago, know what to say to him, today?

"...that this nation shall have a new birth of freedom..."

That's what Casey needed, a new birth of freedom, but how was that going to happen, as long as Mitchell was there to beat him up every day.

During late spring of 2008, French troops began massing in the area of Nancy, France. France attacked Germany early June 2008, in a triangular format. Beginning in Strasbourg, a little French town located on the border, one side of the triangle continued on to Mannheim and Frankfurt, the other side of the triangle continued to Stuttgart and Nuremberg.

In severe fighting, the French captured all five cities and all the resources contained therein the triangle. Germany was completely caught off guard and quickly mobilized all men and machines available to send to quell the attack and defend the country.

"Good evening. This is World News Tonight for June 8th, 2008. In a surprise move, France declared war on Germany today. The French Army invaded Germany at two thirty this afternoon."

The French then settled down after the initial attack to pillage and loot the countryside and enjoy the fruits of their labors. It wasn't long before the French army began to while away the time and enjoy the food and the beer, and especially the women they found available in the fertile German region.

Later the French began to move out of their safe position to begin to swarm into the adjoining countryside, however, during a terrible thunderstorm, the French Army planners and tacticians made a slight miscalculation and a disastrous tactical mistake, and moved in a westerly direction. This of course would take them back toward France.

With the German army behind them culling the rear ranks of unsuspecting French soldiers as they moved west, both armies moved into France. During the ensuing battle, the German army decimated the French army, but French reinforcements arrived during the heaviest of the thunderous downpours and wreaked their havoc upon the German army.

Without knowing it, the French had led the German army into a trap where they were completely surrounded. The German army was completely wiped out to a man, but not without serious and grave losses by the French. Fully ninety five percent of the French army was lost. The media dubbed this rain soaked battle as the "Wet War".

Both countries sent an immediate call out to the people to "Join and Defend" their countries and men came from every city and county to enter military service and fight the oppressors. Both armies were nearly completely annihilated during the "Wet War", and both France and Germany began again after several weeks of preparation.

French citizens, men and women, of the area between Dijon, Nancy, Mulhouse and Strasbourg, picked up all the weapons and dragged or drove all the vehicles to private garages throughout the region to repair and re-use them.

Once the repairs were complete and the rain had stopped, the citizens of the area along with the French soldiers they rescued from the battle, after burying the fallen, re-entered Germany and continued the war, this time more for the chance to avenge their husbands, sons, brothers and fathers who were lost in the war.

Belgium and Luxembourg were caught in the middle and in no time both were completely overrun by both sides. News of the "Wet War" had been all over the Evening News and the Luxembourg government was smart enough to foresee their own impending doom and unconditionally surrendered to the first wave of troops to invade their country. The Belgian government had seen the same news reports and after the Big Fight fiasco, did the same as Luxembourg. Neither Belgium nor Luxembourg had any citizens killed and incurred no damage to even a single building.

The Germans are militarily stronger and historically, better tacticians than the French, but the French spent much more time preparing for this war and thus clearly had the upper hand for a longer time. But with strength and technology on the side of the Germans, this allowed them to invade and occupy large chunks of the French countryside. The maps of the two countries changed so drastically during the years 2008 and 2009 that neither country knew exactly where the borders were for months at a time.

In the third grade, Casey finally got smart enough to accept the opportunity to enroll in a class studying Kung Fu with a neighbor, a noted Kung Fu master that Teresa took him to visit when they were playing outside, one cold Saturday afternoon. It seemed like Casey had a black eye and bruises from the very first time he encountered Mitchell.

Teresa knocked on the door and a small Chinese man of forty-seven opened the door. Mr. Soo is very unassuming looking, standing only five feet five inches tall. He appeared slight of build weighed only one hundred thirty five pounds. His coal black hair and dark eyes added to his mysterious look.

"Mr. Soo, would you please teach my friend Casey how to do Kung Fu?"

"Please come in. Won't you sit here with me? Now then, what is it you wish to do, my boy?" He asked Casey.

Teresa answered for Casey, "There's this boy that goes to school with us, and he beats Casey up just because he takes his books home every day."

"I see Casey is a treasured friend, Miss Teresa. And what of you Master Casey? Are you ready to begin a new life of meditation and discipline?"

Casey wasn't sure what the man was talking about, but if it helped stop Mitch from beating him up every day, it would be worth it.

"Yes Sir."

The Virtual Classroom experience continued in Astronomy. Later, the class will have experiences in Social Studies, Literature, Math, and Physics. Today the class will have the opportunity to watch as Galileo makes his most sensational discovery.

"Galileo made his most sensational discovery in 1610, the four satellites of Jupiter. He named these after the Medici family. The moons Callisto, Ganymede, Europa and Io all have diameters greater than 1900 miles and move about Jupiter in different orbits. That same year he observed the peculiar form of Saturn, however, it's rings were recognized several years later by Huygens."

"But, today we are sitting in a room at the University of Padua, where he taught mathematics. Galileo is gazing into the heavens through a telescope which he invented and built with his own hands. Watch as he first observes the four large moons around the huge planet, Jupiter." Mrs. Velasquez said.

Again the class sat in awe as the famous man stood working before them. Casey was especially entranced with the spectacle he saw there. Astronomy is truly an impressive study, and Casey would not put it away so easily.

The war in Europe continued through the winter and into 2009. The war is wearing on and claiming more and more men and material from the two countries.

With all of the German First Army destroyed and more than ninety five percent of the French Ground Forces lying dead on the fields of France, the French Air Forces were ordered to attack German manufacturing and military bases.

For years, the French Air Force flew the well known French-built Mirage fighters, but five years ago, a young aeronautical engineer came up with a revolutionary new design. The new design has three wings, a canard in the front, a movable main wing and an unusual "A" shaped tail. The plane is extremely maneuverable and although it is under powered, still very fast. The two countries are engaged daily in the air war over central Europe, and planes from both countries were falling out of the sky like ducks during hunting season in the fall.

The Germans had been working on an improved version of the laser rifle, but with the war on German soil, the untested weapon must be pressed into service. They now had reduced its size comparative to an old-time bazooka type gun. Although it was not very heavy, it remained cumbersome and required two men to mount, hold, sight and fire it. It's firepower was devastating to any wheeled vehicle, or for that matter, any pedestrian as well, but still must be improved further if it was to be used on tanks and other armored vehicles. It needed more range and accuracy to be effective with airplanes.

France began this war with a population of sixty million, Germany, seventy million, by 2009, the combined population of the two countries was under one hundred million. Mostly soldiers were the ones killed, and those drafted after the beginning of the hostilities, but a great number of civilians were killed as well. Neither country had any military of any kind left, and not many men either.

"Good evening. This is World News Tonight for September 17th 2009. An earthquake shook the northern mountains of Chile today. The quake registered five point five on the Richter scale and went mostly unnoticed."

"The war in Europe still continues to take lives of the French and German peoples. The war has expanded to Spain and Portugal, Poland and the Czech Republic, Hungary and Romania, and Italy and Austria. It seems like the whole of Europe has gone crazy."

"It has only recently become known that England has been selling arms to many European countries in order to hurry the war along to a conclusion."

Last year Casey learned something from Mr. Soo to stop Mitchell. Casey studied with Mr. Soo every day and had finally perfectedthe one new move that Mr. Soo had taught him. He also learned that he must continue to study and train in order to keep ahead of Mitchell.

Mitchell was much larger and stronger than Casey, but Casey was more cunning. Mitchell heard of Casey's training and decided to confront him about it. It didn't take Casey long to throw Mitchell to the ground. This little demonstration didn't hurt Mitchell, but it did surprise him and he would not let this little black haired heathen do this to him again. Or so he thought.

It had been two weeks since the last news report of hostile action in Europe, when the newly crowned King Charles III took personal charge of the war, and in an armed caravan, drove the short distance from London to Paris, marched into the French Parliament and declared English rule over France then and there.

At that exact time, the English Prime Minister, Benjamin Harris, was standing in the Federal Parliament Building in Bonn declaring those same facts to the German Chancellor and his cabinet. All Ministers and cabinet members of both countries were sent home, and English counterparts were installed that very day in March of 2010.

Once France and Germany had completely pulverized each other during their private little war, English air and ground forces met little or no resistance. During that day, English air and ground forces had landed in every major city and town and had taken control of all military bases located in France and Germany. The super secret laser rifle had been confiscated by the English forces and was thus incorporated into their military arsenal.

In the next few days, King Charles published in the local papers, his idea of the European States to become law as soon as all of the European countries fell into line under English rule. Neither French nor German will be allowed to be spoken or taught anywhere on the continent. English was now the official language of these countries, and all who refused to comply were jailed and dealt with severely.

Spain and Portugal were the next countries in Europe to be visited by Charles and the English forces. Then Switzerland, Luxembourg, Belgium and Holland, all of which gave no resistance whatsoever.

During the next several months of 2010, England cleaned up the war and marched on through Europe taking Italy, Spain, Greece, Poland, Portugal, Belgium, Denmark, Luxembourg, Switzerland, Hungary, Holland, Romania and the Czech Republic. England now controlled all of the European continent to Russia and Turkey on the east.

King Charles had been out in front of his forces as they traveled through each country during the takeover of each country. Two days after the last country, Poland, was taken into the European States by English forces, King Charles III fell from a polo pony and broke his neck, killing him on the spot. His son ascended to the throne as King William V in the ensuing weeks.

England cut up Europe into states, but not according to the original boundaries, more to make all the states nearly equal in size. Using the numbered parallels, the states become squarish and more nearly equal in size to one another. The English Empire now stretched to Russia and Turkey, Africa and the Mediterranean, and the Atlantic. Since all warring countries were conquered now, peace is in sight.

As with all kids, they play with trains, trucks and dolls, they learn to play an instrument and boys are just barely tolerant of girls. But when Casey learned that Teresa was to be taking band class this year, he acquired a sudden interest in learning to play an instrument, any instrument. Fifth grade is tough enough for a young boy, but trying to keep up with a certain girl and his lessons both at the same time is very taxing on the young male libido.

During the first few weeks of band class, the teacher would let any of the new students try their hand at any instrument to see if they had any aptitude there. Casey wasn't very good at music and the teacher, Mr. Bates, asked him to leave several times, but Casey kept coming back to sit next to Teresa during band practice.

"Casey, I thought I asked you to leave this class."

"Yes sir, but I want to play something."

"What would you like to play?"

"Uh, - the, uh, - guitar?" Casey said.

"I am sorry, but there is no guitar in the band."

"Well, how about the, uh, - banjo?"

"No, not the banjo either."

"OK, uh, - maybe the trumpet?" Casey said.

Try as he would, Casey couldn't play the trumpet either. But Mr. Bates could see what instrument Casey had his eye on and he allowed him to hold the chimes and sit there by Teresa if he would agree to be quiet.

"Casey, you sit there until I point at you to play."

Mr. Bates, of course, had no intention on ever pointing at Casey for him to play. After several weeks of being quiet and sitting next to Teresa and basking in his nearness to her, finally Mr. Bates allowed Casey to play the chimes which he did not completely stink at while playing. Mr. Bates agreed to teach him the guitar during a non-band class period.

The latest toy craze for the younger kids was Holopet, Holofriend and Holofoe. The toy was worn on the wrist like a wrist watch and the child could use buttons on the side of the watch face to control it. A hologram of your pet, friend or foe stood three inches above the wrist, and was controlled with the several buttons.

"Good evening. This is World News Tonight for July 18th, 2010. General of the Army of Libya, Muman Akbar was an eye witness to an attempted coup in that country today, and is speaking with us now. General Akbar, can you tell us exactly what has happened?"

"Two men approached our sovereign leader and I as we were standing together in the Capital Building today. Both of these cowardly men drew their weapons and shot our leader four times and ran out into the street. I have seen these men before and we will catch and kill them. I have temporarily taken control of the country, and I do believe that the coup was thwarted even though our beloved leader was killed."

Chapter 3

Muman Akbar

July 2010

A few days after the assassination, there was a knock at the side door of the general's dwelling.

"We have come as you have ordered, Your Excellency."

"Quickly! Inside! You must not be seen here!"

The two men hurried into the palace and sat where they were told.

"Here is the money I promised you, and here is your travel money. You will go this very night to Baghdad to my cousin, Fatin Hassan. He is the Minister of Defense there and deliver this letter. You will do for him what you have done for me, then you will disappear, forever. And I warn you, if even one word of this is ever heard by a single living soul, you will know that I am behind you with my knife at your heart."

Early in January of the next year, after General Akbar had assumed power and installed some of his friends and relatives to high positions in government, he contacted the United States for a meeting with the President in Washington DC

It became a media event with the two Presidents shaking hands and smiling, and uttering phrases of affection for all to hear. Muman Akbar knew exactly how to smile for the cameras and the Americans. Speaking through his smiles, he promised a new beginning of Arab-American relations

The Libyan-American talks continued for two more days, with all concerned smiling and shaking hands for the cameras, and each other. President Akbar had promised to sell oil to the United States and allow ships to call into port at both Benghazi and Tripoli. He had announced that he was now a "US Partner".

Shortly after the end of the meeting, the US President's Press Secretary, Larry Campbell, was asked during the press conference, "What do you think of the new Libyan President, Larry?"

"Well, he must be a pretty good guy, his name means 'trustworthy' in the Arabic language."

"Good evening. This is World News Tonight for January 24th 2011. "General Muman Akbar, the Libyan President, has today concluded talks with President Kratzer which included much discourse about trade and cooperation. The Libyan President has said that he wants Libya to embrace the Americans more, and become trading partners. He told one reporter, "You don't have to call me General, just Muman. I'm just a regular guy like you."

Muman Akbar spent the next four months in meetings with Egypt, Iraq, Iran, Jordan and Lebanon to explain his plan to get money from the United States. All of the heads of state whom he met and talked with agreed to go along with the plan except Iran and Iraq.

Akbar traveled to each of the Arab countries, saying, "This is a time we must make our governments stable. What better way that with money supplied from our enemy, the West."

General Akbar has traveled to Iraq three times and offered a coalition to Iraq based on his plan to acquire US dollars, but the leader of Iraq loudly and flatly refused. The leader of Iraq said publicly while Muman was visiting Baghdad on Iraqi TV that "This pretender who has dared to presume to lead the great country of Libya has brought great shame upon all Muslim nations because of his actions. He works for the forces of darkness."

General Akbar was incensed at the accusations of this old dictator and after he witnessed public hangings and gruesome torture in Iraq and decided then and there that the ruler must be replaced. It appears cousin Fatin's plan must begin immediately.

Actually all Akbar wanted was American aid, the kind you can spend. Unfortunately, Iran and their leadership, Muhammad Abdullah Habib, President of Iran, were against his plan as well, and he was escorted out of the country by the Iranian Police. Habib has accused Akbar of consorting with the enemy and crimes too numerous to mention.

Muman Akbar had too many huge goals to let little things like this stop or set him back. There are always other ways to achieve your goals, even if those ways are slightly immoral or illegal.

"We have been summoned by the Minister of Defense, Most High." One of the men said.

"Enter! Guard, take these two men to the Minister of Defense and stay with them until he dismisses you."

The guard escorted the two men down the hall to an office and the three of them entered the office.

"These two men say that you have sent for them, Minister."

One of the men handed a letter to the minister, which he opened and quickly read.

"Yes, these men are here to see me. You may go now."

Once the guard had left and the three men had retreated to the Minister's private office, he spoke. "How is my cousin and what of your homeland?"

"The President is well and sends his regards. We have been sent to you to help solve your problem, but we would like to be paid now, if you please."

The Minister placed a goatskin bag on the table and one of the men took it and spilled its contents of gold coins and jewels onto the table.

"When will you do the job?"

"Within the week, Minister. Soon they will be calling you 'Your Excellency'."

The three of them enjoyed a laugh and the two men left by a side door.

"Good evening. This is World News Tonight for February 22 2011. Minister of Defense of Iraq, Fatin Hassan was with the Iraqi leader when he collapsed last night, and is speaking with us now. Minister Hassan, can you tell us exactly what has happened?"

"Our beloved sovereign leader and I were standing together in the Capital Building last night when he clutched his chest and collapsed to the floor. He was rushed to the nearest hospital, but had expired before the doctors could examine him. The doctors have reported to me that he died from exposure to an unknown virus. I have temporarily taken control of the country until stability can be achieved."

Soon all the male members of the family arrived in Baghdad to help their cousin Fatin. His father, uncles, brothers, brothers in law and even their grandfathers offered their expert help.

President Muhammad Abdullah Habib, of Iran had been told by his spies and confidants that there had been antagonism generated by Muman Akbar of Libya toward all of the surrounding nations of the Middle East after the assassination of their leader and now the leader of Iraq. This of course was untrue. Muman was busily working on his plan, but it had annoyed Muhammad Habib to a boiling point. Finally, Habib refused to listen to any more of what his spies called Akbar's "drivel" which the Iranian news media said Akbar spouted, and Iran attacked Libya in all out war.

Fortunately, Cousin Fatin Hassan has spies also, and they reported to him on September 25th, 2011 that all Iranian planes would attack at once that day. Fatin called Muman to alert him to the impending invasion.

"You have only minutes! You must act now!" And act he did.

Libya was flying the French Mirage 2000A, known as the "A" Plane, built by Dassault-Breguet. It was the fastest plane in the Middle East. It carried two SNECMA turbofan engines making 10,000 kg of thrust for that little plane. When the main wings are in the attack position, the plane could approach 2000 mph in flight.

Iran was flying Russian made MIG-35 fighters. Built by Mikoyan-Gurevich, and using two of the Lyulka turbojet engines, they developed 20,000 kg of thrust and the plane was far more powerful than the "A" Plane. The problem was that the little "A" Plane could fly circles around the bigger Russian plane.

Iraq was flying the Russian Sukhoi Su-29 fighters, it carried two Tumansky turbojets with 6500 kg of thrust, much heavier and slower than either of the other planes. These sand colored planes with the unusual triangular patch stood out in the blue sky. Iraq's markings were quite unusual for that part of the world, when all the other national aircraft markings are circular, Iraq had a green triangle with a black border and two vertical red diamonds on the sides and wings of their planes.

Unknown to either of the combatants, President Khalid Barakah, of Eqypt has a plan of his own, which had not been published. A simple plan.

"Call General Zafir immediately."

The secretary picked up the phone and made the call. Twenty seven minutes later General Zafir entered the office of the President.

"You called, Excellency?"

"Yes General. Soon there will be planes of three warring countries flying over our land. You will know these planes by their markings, the black circle with a green dot in the center and a red border, and the white circle with red center and green border and a green triangle with a black border and two vertical red diamonds."

"When these planes are seen by our spotters or our radar, shoot them down. Once the planes stop flying, take your Air Force and eliminate all planes found on the ground of these three countries. Then continue to eliminate any other threat from other countries as quickly as you can."

Israel will watch the war from a distance and prepare for the war's end.

Teresa and her best friend, Betty were walking home together one night in October, and Teresa confided in her that she really liked Casey.

"I know that already, Teresa. Casey is the only one in our sixth grade class that doesn't know that." The two of them giggled the rest of the way home about Casey.

Casey found out that the local Boy Scout leader was a rancher there in AJ and he had horses. Casey always wanted to learn to ride a horse and now he had an opportunity. Teresa always seemed to be around on the weekends and after school and tonight was no exception. Casey ran into his house and threw down his books and ran back out to get his bike.

"Where ya goin' Casey?" she asked.

"To Boy Scouts."

"Can I go with you?"

"You're not a boy, you silly girl."

"I'll just ride along to keep you company, OK?"

"OK - - - I guess." He droned.

They rode through the streets to the dirt road leading to Mr. Castilla's ranch and out the mile and a half to the house.

Casey could see the corral around the side of the house as they rode up to the front, and he went straight for it. There was a swayback old brown standing in the corral, and as the two kids walked to the fence, Mortimer, looked through the wood rail fence at them.

Casey reached up and Mortimer obliged him by bending down so Casey could pet his nose. Teresa knew that if Casey could do it, she could too, but Mortimer got a whiff of the perfume she was wearing for Casey, and snorted on her hand and scared her. Of course, Casey didn't notice anything but the horse snorting. Casey still must get his sensitivity and his nose trained, if ever.

Casey was very busy now, he had his martial arts training, homework every day, he had just taken up horseback riding and even though he doesn't know it yet, he had a new girlfriend.

It was a short war, Muman Akbar of Libya had a lot of bravado and Muhammad Abdullah Habib of Iran had a lot of anger, but neither had a lot of military might. Egypt on the other hand did have and overran both Libya and Iran and all of the countries between except Israel. All the Arab states dislike Israel, but none of them are willing to take Israel on in a war.

Once Egypt had the middle eastern countries brought into line, it was easy to conquer and rule all of Africa that Egypt wanted. The Egyptians has long been known for their solid reputation as builders and thinkers, and who better to bring the Middle East together into a cohesive unit.

Akbar was made Liaison to the West by the Egyptian President, Khalid Barakah, the Iranian President was killed, and Fatin was praised by Eqypt for his understanding and reserve in this matter. Country by country, Egypt took over all of north Africa and the middle east including Libya, Iran and Iraq.

Teresa's mother has agreed to Teresa's first boy-girl birthday party this year, she was thirteen now. Teresa invited Casey and all her best friends from school and church, but not Mitchell. Mitchell was always mean to Casey, and Teresa doesn't like him for that. Teresa likes Casey too much for that.

The party was set for Saturday after her real birthday on Thursday. There will be games like volleyball and basketball and pizza for everyone. This one was a day time party only, it ended at five in the afternoon, but in January, it was already dark at five o'clock.

Casey was finally beginning to get his homework done in school now, which allowed him more time for the other things, like band class with Teresa and the Boy Scouts. The Boy Scouts was teaching him survival in an unfriendly land. The great southwest can be unfriendly all year round, and learning to handle guns and recognize dangers is a mandatory course.

Learning everything about the outdoors has always been a must for boys and girls too. There are too many dangers like snakes, scorpions and even poison plants to be aware of. Teresa was there with him every day, helping him and learning along with him in everything he does.

The paloverde tree grows in the southwest along the sides of desert canyons and dry ditches in southern and central Arizona and it is the Arizona state tree. It grows fifteen to thirty feet high and as much as twenty inches in diameter. It is covered with green bark and leaves in March and April, the leaves fall to the ground during late May and are replaced by yellow flowers, the tree is bare the rest of the year.

The Mesquite tree, also common to southwest, may grow fifty to sixty feet tall, with a trunk up to three feet in diameter. It becomes full with leaves and provides shade in hot dry areas. Both of these trees grow in gullies and arroyos found in central and south Arizona.

The saguaro or giant cactus grows to be fifty feet high and two and one half feet in diameter with flowers on the tips of branches and stems. The cholla or jumping cactus has been given a false reputation for leaping at passers-by because its thorny branches break off easily and cling to people and animals.

The spines cause painful wounds and it usually takes another person the help pull the thorns out since they are barbed like fish hooks. Later Casey and Teresa will learn about the cactus called prickly pear, organ-pipe and barrel cactus.

People have always wanted space where no one else lives close to them, but since 2000, crime in the cities has increased, since 2005 it has increased even more, and now it was increasing at an alarming rate. Because of this increase, real estate agents from all up and down the east coast have been advertising land in every hollow, canyon, and all the nooks and crannies up and down the Appalachian Mountains for sale.

When these agents tell the people living in the backwoods about all the millions of dollars that they can make by selling their land to the stupid un-suspecting "city-folk", greed set in and sales went through the roof. The one thing that was not men-tioned, was that the agents would make most of the money by over-charging fees with a little swindling thrown in for good measure.

As road rage escalated and crime increased and jobs decreased, living in the cities became much more dangerous. More and more people longed for the peace and serenity of an old-fashioned log house, or a new fashioned berm house. More and more people were leaving the cities for the wilderness, they were living in everything from caves and underground houses to log and cement faced earthen sheltered houses.

The population of all the little towns increased in proportion to the influx of people from the big cities. They moved to Hawley and Lykens, Romney and Upper Tract, Goshen and Sweet Springs, Dublin and New Land, Ingalls and Maggie, and Erwin and Etowah.

The Appalachian Mountains were a good place to hide if that's what you wanted to do. There are trees of maple, ash, oak, cherry and apple. But there was one group that it has always been impossible to hide from, the US Government.

Word came down from the Secretary of the Interior: "Send someone out there to find out what is going on, this sounds serious. We need to know what the reason is that all these people have left the cities, and how to get them to come back to the workforce in the cities." The letter from the Secretary was passed around like a hot potato, until it showed up one day on the desk of the Director of the Internal Revenue Service.

"What is this, Wilson?"

Fredrick Wilson, the Director's aide explained what had been happening and tried to interpret the Secretary's letter, but the Director had a vision. If he can accomplish this task, it will put a feather in his cap and the Administration will look favorably upon him. The Director is an idiot.

"Wilson, send some of our agents out into the field to talk to these people and get me some answers."

By the time the order was sent out to the field, interpreted and reinterpreted by supervisors and administrators, the field agents were told "do not take any bull" and "be careful, these people are radicals". The government has a unique way of distorting and rearranging the facts to suit the Government's purposes.

The IRS agents acted like cowboys fighting the Indians in a "B" movie. Many agents were killed when they started confrontations for no apparent reason.

One bright sunny Saturday morning, an IRS agent knocked on a door in eastern Tennessee with his pistol drawn. When the neighbor who was standing in his yard next door asked the agent what he wanted, the agent turned and fired two shots at him. The agent's aim was off a little and when he sneezed, and he shot the neighbor's dog as the neighbor dove for cover.

Not knowing who had knocked at his front door, and what the shots were for. The owner of the house, Samuel Johnson, who had heard the commotion and grabbed his gun on his way to answer the door, pumped three bullets into the agent just as the agent turned his gun toward him in an effort to shoot him also. The agent was dead where he fell.

"Who is this guy anyway?" Sam Johnson asked as Alex Petrof, his neighbor walked up. "What's he shootin' at us for?"

The two of them rummaged through his pockets and found the agents badge and ID, which were still in his wallet in his hip pocket.

"Good evening, this is World News Tonight for July 11, 2013. An earthquake registering six point one on the Richter scale shook the southern mountains of Peru last night. Causing a landslide which totally filled one end of a canyon, blocking a stream flowing there. Now there is a reservoir filling up behind the earthen dam. Local natives will soon have more water for their use."

"In this unusual item. IRS agents have been reportedly attacking citizens on their property and in their houses. There have been reports of shootings from West Virginia to Florida. Twenty five IRS agents and forty four citizens have been shot and killed during the last twenty four hours."

"No one has found the reason why the agent was standing on Mr. Johnson's porch or why the agent had his pistol drawn and ready to shoot Mr. Johnson. An autopsy will be conducted to help with any additional questions that may come up."

When Casey and Teresa were thirteen, they rode their bikes to Mr. Castilla's place and borrowed the two horses they had been learning to ride for the past year. They rode off into the canyons and arroyos of the Superstition Mountains.

It was always just the two of them when they rode, they would walk or ride close together and hold hands. But this time was different, Teresa had been high spirited like her horse all day and when they stopped under the shade of one of the huge paloverde trees and take a drink of water from their canteen, she pantsed him. Then she stood there and pointed and looked and laughed at him.

Casey, being the normal thirteen-year-old that he was, wouldn't take that without a payback, and he did the same to her and they both laughed. The two of them stood there with their pants around their ankles, pointing and looking and laughing at each other. Teresa moved to Casey and put her arms around him and kissed him lightly on the lips.

"What are you doing?" He asked as he pulled back from her.

"I'm just telling you that I like you." She said as she moved her hands over his strong body.

"Oh, you want to get funny." He said.

"You know that you have to marry me now, don't you?" She said after a few minutes looking at him.

"Why?"

"Because I'm yours now, you own me. Now I can be with no one for the rest of my life."

"No one?" He asked.

"Do you love me?" She asked.

"Yes."

"Will you marry me?" She asked.

"Yes."

"Good!" She said.

"When can we do it?" He asked.

"When you have a job to support me." She said.

"A job! You want me to have a job?" He said as if stunned by her exclamation.

"Yes you fool, and I want diamonds and pearls and stacks and stacks of money." She said and laughed, then he laughed. They both jumped up, adjusted their clothes and rode on back to town. They always had a good time together.

Chapter 4

Faces and Places

July 2014

Just as the war in Europe had ended quickly after the consolidation of all the conquered lands into one complete country, the war in the Middle East ended in the same way after Egypt consolidated the Arab Nations together. Within a few months after the United Arab States of Egypt (UASE) became a reality, China began to feel the same warring urges that afflicted the others before them.

In July of 2014, China's Chairman, Chung Chishen and Vice Chairman, Wong Liushing mounted an army of over one million soldiers into three huge armies which started south taking every square inch of land in their path. The Chinese armies began to move south like a swarm of ants, devouring everything in their path, slowly, methodically, relentlessly, incessantly the armies moved across the southern border of China into unsuspecting foreign nations.

Neighboring countries began to fall like dominoes in three separate lines. The largest of the three armies, half a million men, commanded by General Xiang Leelok moved into Vietnam, Laos, and Burma. All who resisted were slaughtered, the decree was sent out that Chinese is the official language of all countries and people, or death. It was only a few months before the advancing army crossed into Thailand and Kampuchea. Word spread quickly of the army and their ruthless behavior into Maylaysia and Sumatra and the Chinese army followed quickly behind the rumors. It would not take long to complete the takeover of Borneo, The Philippines and New Guinea.

Egypt captured the desalinization equipment from Libya during the takeover operation and soon fresh, desalinized water began to flow into a low part of the desert, making a new lake on the border of Libya and Egypt. The water was running twenty-four hours a day for months. Finally the new lake began to take shape, slowly, but it was there for all to behold, a new lake in the middle of the Sahara Desert for all to see. It was only a short time before tents and agricultural beginnings were there as well.

In August an HIV patient was cured, but there is no known cure for this disease. Jeffrey Watson had contracted the HIV virus from bad blood given by a skid row bum who needed money for another bottle of wine. The blood was not checked for the virus and when Jeff had a surgical procedure done in the hospital, he was given the blood. Of course, he had no idea that the blood was tainted with the virus, and when several months later, he was told by his doctor that he was HIV positive, Jeff was furious. His fury grew into rage and the rage that he felt wouldn't go away. It grew with every passing day and one Saturday night he stopped in to a local bar to try to drink the rage away.

"Gimme a shot and a beer."

"Comin' right up."

Jeff drank the first two quickly and ordered a third. He picked up the beer and threw his money on the bar and walked toward the pool table.

"I'll take the winner." he said and put his money on the pool table.

Soon the game in progress was over and it was Jeff's turn to play. The beer wasn't doing what he had hoped for, the rage continued to grow and now fueled with alcohol, Jeff's judgment was impaired as well. Halfway through the game, another player accidentally bumped him, which was the straw that broke the camels back with Jeff's frenzy. Jeff hit him with the cue stick, a big mistake.

"What the hell you think you're doin'?" The other player said as he got up from the floor and punched Jeff in the face.

The man Jeff had hit with the cue stick was a regular at the bar and several of his friends were there to help him. Jeff got the worst of the rest of the fight, but not before breaking a chair over one man's head and throwing the six ball through the front window after his real target ducked.

The bartender dialed 911 and yelled into the phone. "This is Kilroy's bar, I got a guy here breakin' up the place! Get a cop over here, quick!"

It wasn't long before the Prince William County Police were taking charge of the bar, the fight and Jeff. Jeff got to wear a brand new pair of handcuffs and got his first free ride in a police car to the hospital.

"Bring him in here guys."

"Good evening. This is World News Tonight for August 23rd 2014. In Woodbridge, Virginia, a man, Jeffrey Watson, was brought into Potomac Hospital by police after a fight in a bar. After setting his broken arm and jaw, a blood test was performed on Mr. Watson since his doctor, Doctor Enoch Zimmer, was there in the hospital treating another patient. Dr. Zimmer said that he checked Watson last Thursday and Dr. Zimmer was sure he had the HIV virus at that time, and that the test was positive. However the blood test was negative today. Mr. Watson has agreed to stay in the hospital while the doctors run a few more tests. Mr. Watson was very docile and cooperative once he was received into the hospital emergency room."

Teresa and Casey were now together constantly, either riding their bikes around town or Mr. Castilla's horses into the desert, or at school functions, or studying every book they could lay their hands on. Both of them were voracious when it came to learning something new.

The weekend before school started was a big rodeo at the Fort McDowell Indian Reservation and Teresa and Casey were happy to go. Teresa participated in the barrel racing and was pretty good at it. Casey fancied himself a bronc rider, but he never quite got the hang of it. He had always been able to ride with the best of them, but the broncs could put him on the ground without half trying.

Teresa took Casey to meet her grandfather, Judge, and an aunt and uncle after the rodeo was over. Her family were glad to see her and even more glad to see that she brought "such a nice young man" with her. Her grandfather told them stories and explained many new things to the two kids. They talked for hours about snakes and scorpions, guns and knives, and Cherokee lore.

"Do you like my little Teresa, Casey?" Judge asked.

"Yes sir, I do." Casey said.

"Do you take her to dances and movies?"

"Yes sir. There's a Halloween dance coming soon that we will attend."

"Is he good to you my dear?"

"Yes grandfather, he is, and I love him a lot." Teresa said.

Egypt began to dig a canal during the spring of 2015, big enough for small freighters to navigate from the Red Sea through the Gulf of Aqaba northward toward the Dead Sea. The canal allowed water to flow from the gulf into the Dead Sea area.

The Dead Sea was at a level of four hundred feet below sea level before the construction began, and it took quite a long time to fill this large void. Once the water filled all of the lowest areas, it overflowed into a valley in Jordan near the town of Al Karak, making a new lake there. Now Egypt has a new water route directly to Jordan and Mesopotamia. Soon ships will be calling into the middle of the Syrian Desert.

The second Chinese Army commanded by General Lin Ganyu moved into Korea, Japan and Taiwan in the same manner as the others. The Third Army commanded by General Leung Faiho moved into Bhutan and Nepal. These peoples found the same treatment from the army and one by one, the countries fell under Chinese control. Next came Bangladesh and Pakistan and last was India.

April 14 2015 will stand out in history as one of the worst days in the history of the United States of America. Unknown to anyone on Wall Street, the fail-safe set years before to prevent severe movement of the Dow Jones, somehow overloaded the computer and the computer crashed. The Dow dropped five thousand points before close of business.

Technicians were working feverishly through the day and on into the night to find some glimmer of hope to rescue the financial marketplace. What they found was the backup files were corrupted and something happened to throw the computer off line. By the time the main computer was back on line all the files in the system were corrupted and the fail-safe itself failed this time and the main computer system fell off line to stay.

It was a cascade effect with the banking institutions, soon it affected the banks in and around New York, then New Jersey and Pennsylvania. The crash soon was spreading up and down the east coast and then west into the country.

In only a few weeks, companies were laying off workers because they had no money for payrolls. People had no money for rent and food and shelters and mission were overflowing with homeless people. More and more companies laid off more and more workers and many companies closed their doors.

The depression spread mass unemployment, poverty and despair throughout the country, as well as our neighbors to the north and south. Suddenly there were no jobs, no money and no food. Prices are down, but no one can buy anything since there isn't money to spend. The newspapers continue to harp that tired old line, "It's just like the Great Depression of 1929." How would they know if they had no basis in fact of this comparison?

The entire country was plunged into a black hole of financial distress like none before. Bank failures wiped out savings of nearly all of the blue collar workers around the country. People could not make their rent and mortgage payments and millions of homes were repossessed, on paper, but the banks and mortgage companies had already gone under and these institutions had no workers to claim the repossessions.

It was a long miserable summer for most of the country. The MacKenzies and the Basillios didn't have much to start with, so they weren't hit as hard as others with a lot to lose. Both families were put out of work, but that had happened before and they felt they could ride it out again.

Teresa and Casey would be entering tenth grade at Superstition Mountain High School in September, but all during the summer they had been riding in the mountains, studying the trees and the cactus and at night studying the stars and watching the sparkling lights in the sky. Casey said they were studying astronomy, but while Teresa was looking at the stars,

Casey was looking at her. Teresa is smarter than he thinks and as soon as school began, she made a visit to the school library.

"Look Casey, I found a book on Astronomy at the library. I've always been interested in the stars and the skies."

"Yeah, me too."

Teresa kept the book checked all during that school year, and the two of them read the book and searched the heavens for each of the stars and planets seen from the northern hemisphere until they could find them without the book's help.

"Those lights that we see every night in the northern sky, Casey, I think it's the Aurora Borealis. The book says that electrically charged particles makes the lights at the north pole if the conditions are right and we can see them from here. I wonder why we can see them every day, though. This is really interesting, Monday I'm going to find out some more about this."

Paper currency printed by the government prior to the change of the millennium became worthless and was removed from circulation shortly after the crash. Since paper money could be easily counterfeited and the process was becoming more popular with criminals, and coins are much more difficult to duplicate, coins were back in style.

Therefore, coins of every shape and size suddenly came into circulation and coin operated devices of every kind were back in style. However, only the cheapest metals, such as copper and nickel, were being used to mint coins, another everyday reminder of the graft and corruption prevalent from the lowest to the highest in the government.

One bright spot to the new coin craze, was that robberies were down since the great weight of coins made robberies and muggings more trouble that they were worth.

The government minted round copper coins in five cent, ten cent, twenty-five cent, and one dollar denominations, using the established dies currently in use by the mint. These round coins have Thomas Jefferson in the five cent piece, Franklin Roosevelt on the ten cent piece, George Washington on the twenty-five cent piece and Dwight Eisenhower on the one dollar piece.

New hexagonal coins for five, ten and twenty dollar coins were minted in nickel with the Washington Monument on the five dollar coin, the Statue of Liberty on the ten dollar coin, and the White House on the twenty dollar coin. Very large octagonal coins were made of lead with Congress on the fifty dollar coin and Mount Rushmore on the one hundred dollar coin.

Slang for money soon became "Faces and Places", and since faces are one dollar and less and places are five dollars and up, working people only saw the faces.

The biggest joke around the country with those people old enough to remember the good times of the nineteen nineties soon became the story about the man on the street begging for money for food and a man hands him a twenty dollar coin. The beggar looked at the coin and said, "Thanks, buddy! What am I going to get for a nickel?"

All gold and silver has been taken out of circulation by the US Government, however gold and silver jewelry, diamonds and other precious stones are still in the hands of the populace, and there is nothing the government can do about it. People soon found that these kinds of treasures are more valuable than all other.

Not all of the banks closed, only the smaller ones. The large banks put most of their people out of work, but managed to keep their doors open. There was not much business for the banks since no one believed in the banks anymore and no one had any money to put into the banks anyway. The farmers had food because they grew it, but they had no money, and bartering became a way of life again.

China now conquered and controlled everything from Russia on the north to Australia on the south and the Pacific ocean to the west. The Chinese had many of the same ideas that the English and the Egyptians had, however, many of the peoples living in the Southeast Asia area spoke more than one language, and one of them was usually Chinese. Policing such an idea would become fruitless for the Chinese.

"Good evening. This is World News Tonight for January 14th, 2016. Photos of a blue planet have arrived from far off space, scientists are working feverishly trying to find a match against the star maps to locate the planet. We are talking with Charles Praeger of NASA. Mr. Praeger, what can you tell us about this new discovery?"

"Decades earlier, the United States sent an explorer probe on it's way into space and forgot all about it. This little probe has been sending signals back to earth all this time but all the pictures were thought to be of no use until now. Now all of those old photos must be recovered from the NASA archives and studiously scrutinized to plot the path of this wandering explorer in order to find a clue to the location of the blue planet. This will take an immense amount of time and effort, but the benefits could be phenomenal."

During the summer, Teresa competed in the barrel racing in the rodeos around the area and Casey tried to achieve a level of competence in bronc riding. He did pretty good on Mr. Castilla's ranch when there was a horse to break, but the broncs in the rodeo just seem to have his number.

At the end of the first week of school, Teresa and Casey were sitting under their favorite paloverde tree talking and holding hands.

"Doesn't the sky look strange Casey? Sort of yellow."

"Yeah, you're right it does."

They both strained to get a good look, the sky indeed did look strange and with good reason. What they could not see was a cloud of dust and other particles was moving in the jet stream slowly almost imperceptibly around the globe.

Casey went out for football as a receiver and unlike his rodeo talents, he was very good at this endeavor.

He could catch the ball no matter who threw it and how badly it was thrown. A player with this kind of ability is known to have "soft hands". The coach only looked at Casey for a few plays and he knew he had his prize winning receiver.

Football season was fun for Casey because the school was winning and Teresa was always close by as a new cheerleader, encouraging him to improve himself. The one dark spot was that Mitchell made the team too, as backup quarterback. Mitchell has grown to hate Casey with a passion, but he can't do anything about it as long as Casey can win every fight that Mitchell starts.

Teresa and Casey were looking forward to the Junior Prom all year, but both of them had one serious problem in common. They were broke. Always broke. Both families had been out of work for about a year and there wasn't any extra money for things like dances. But there was a bright side to even this dark development, Maria was very good with the sewing machine and spent most of the winter making a beautiful dress for her equally beautiful daughter.

Casey, on the other hand, was presented the suit that his father wore to his wedding, by his father. Even though it was twenty years old it has not been worn but that one time.

What will these two kids do? There was no money for gas for the cars, or any other transportation.

"I have an idea! Let's ride our bikes to school and change in the restrooms. We can take our clothes in a suitcase and no one will know any different, but don't tell. Then we can ride home together later."

Casey had to agree, without a plan they wouldn't get to go at all, so he agreed even though he hated the plan.

Later in the evening while they were on the dance floor, he asked her, "You're really loving this aren't you?"

"Yes aren't you?"

"As long as I'm with you, I can endure almost anything, even my dad's old suit."

It seemed like the Arizona Republic newspaper was reporting more instances of the HIV virus being cured on a regular basis. There were articles in the paper showing three reports this fall, one from France, one from Italy and one in the UASE.

It was a long year for the Democratic and Republican nominees and November would be the end of it. Greg Scott ran hard all year long and was rewarded by a big vote and the election as President of the United States. He had his hands full, a major depression, loss of confidence in the government and the banking industry and just plain dissatisfaction with everything in general. But he said he would take charge and put the country back on the right track.

It was February 5th, only a few days after the inauguration in January, that President Scott took a trip to wall street to tour the New York Stock Exchange and confer with the people that knew the most about the problem. It was eerie in that huge empty building. There were only a few people there, the head of the Stock Exchange, a few engineers and technicians, the President and his Secret Service detail and not another voice to be heard.

"A virus was somehow picked up, we think from a computer game, and found it's way to the main computer and corrupted all the files in the mainframe. We have removed and reinstalled all memory devices, disks, tapes everything. We have installed new updated anti virus software and purged all the drives, all we need now is the original program and we can get the show on the road. We have been searching each and every desk and file cabinet for that package of the original product."

It didn't take long for Greg Scott to roll up his sleeves and help them search.

"You guys might as well search too. There's no one here to make an assault on the President." he said to the Secret Service detail.

After two more hours of pulling out drawers of desks and file cabinets, one of the agents stumbled onto the package in a filing cabinet.

"Is this anything?" he said holding it up for a technician to see.

"That's it!"

It was an unblemished copy of both the main program and the fail-safe software hidden away in a drawer marked "Program Files" exactly where it should have been. The technicians ran to the computer and in another hour, the software was loaded and the system came up as if nothing had happened. Now the technicians would work to fix everything in that huge system and get the stock exchange back in operation. It would take much longer than they had hoped.

"Good evening. This is World News Tonight for June 4th, 2017. An earthquake coincided with the eruption of Volcano de Galeras in Colombia. The last time this volcano was active was in 1993. Streams of molten magma are running down the southeast face of the mountain threatening the city of Pasto. The tremor shook Pasto at the same time residents saw the fiery beginnings of the volcano's activity. All residents have been ordered to evacuate their homes and leave the city."

Rodeo, horses and Teresa were the thoughts that pervaded Casey's mind during the summer, and as in the past, Teresa did well in the barrel racing events. Her best for the summer was one first and one second while Casey struggled to achieve only one third place, all his other events were much lower in the standings.

"I don't think you should think of bronc riding as your life's work, Casey. I love you a lot, but you should turn your attention elsewhere."

Teresa giggled when she said it and Casey knew it was the truth.

Finally! They were seniors!

Teresa went out for the cheerleader squad again to be close to Casey and made the squad. She was pretty and athletic and persistent enough to be good at it. Casey again made the football team as the starting receiver and Mitchell was the starting quarterback for the team this year.

"I wonder what Mitchell does during the summer and at nights during the school year, we never see him out on a date or anything." Teresa mused.

The Commuter copter was invented by a man, Fred Goss, who found a way to power a motor with only salt water, his company built the CC for a year. Fred has worked on this for a long time and finally figured it out, during the year Fred built a hundred cars made of space age unbreakable plastic and kept one for himself.

Fred's new Commuter copter will be in one showroom in Phoenix in October of 2017. Fred was hoping to sell fifty or so and maybe it would catch on in Tucson and Flagstaff. Much to Fred's pleasure and satisfaction, the CC was an instant hit with the commuting public in the Phoenix area and sales went through the roof by his standards. Not many people have money for a car, for that matter, not many people have money for anything, but he sold a hundred by Christmas and had orders for a hundred more that he couldn't fill.

It was the last football game of the season, with SMHS one win away from an undefeated season and Casey caught the winning touchdown pass. As Casey was jumping around in the end zone, all the players and cheerleaders ran to him and everyone slapped and hugged each other, but Mitchell stood his ground from the very spot he had thrown the pass and acted like this sort of thing was an everyday occurrence. It was only a minute or two before a camera and microphone were pointed at Mitchell.

"Mitchell, you realize that this win means that you have won the right to play in the State Championship Tournament next week." The reporter said.

"Yes I do, and I believe we will do well because I will be at the helm of this team again and if all the players do their job as well as I have, I believe that we will win." Mitchell said.

"Don't you think that Casey was the main instrumental player in this win tonight?" He said.

"Actually, no. I threw that pass so well that anybody could have caught it, even him."

SMHS won their first game to put them into the quarter finals, but then they came up against the toughest team they had ever faced and lost twenty one to seven. This devastating loss put them out of the running for the state title.

"It was your fault we lost that game, we should be State Champs." Mitchell was yelling at Casey again. Something he had been doing for twelve years now. "I'll get you for this!" Casey had heard it all before.

About once each year every year since the beginning of school, Mitchell tried to beat up Casey in a fight and their senior year was no exception. Connecting the school with the new gymnasium was a long enclosed hallway with three steps to the lower level that was the last bit of concrete poured before the contract was finished.

Later that week Mitchell was hiding in wait at the far end of the hall for Casey and ran down the long hall trying to catch Casey off guard as he entered the gym. Casey has studied with Mr. Soo for ten years now and a little thing like a charging rhino could not beat him.

Casey sidestepped the charging Mitchell as he nearly broke the doors to the gym down when he plummeted through them. Mitchell fought with Casey in the gym. No, that's not quite right. Mitchell swarmed all over Casey, but Casey wasn't there when Mitchell swung his huge lumbering punches, and he never hit Casey once. When Mitchell finally wore himself out as he usually did, Casey threw him onto the floor and Mitchell was too tired to get up. All the football and basketball players were standing around watching the fight and saw Mitchell lose again.

"Mitch, why don't you give up this vendetta you have with Casey, you can't beat him. Why not shake and be friends. He is our best receiver and he catches everything you throw at him except your fists."

"I'll get you for that!" Mitchell screamed as he stormed out of the gym.

"He's always saying that."

In February, the big three auto companies made Fred Goss a huge offer plus royalties for his design, drawings and patent for the Commuter copter. Fred's CC was primarily designed for people to get to work and back and little shopping errands, but the big car companies have other, more grandiose ideas.

Fred's CC had no tail, there was a rear stabilizer fan at the end of a short trunk-like portion, and the main rotor blades fold up when parked by using a handle inside the cab. Using another handle inside, four little wheels came out when on land to power the CC from the landing circle in the parking lot to a parking space and back to the takeoff circle when it was time to depart.

Fred's Instructions to drive his invention seemed pretty simple.

1. Use the key in the ignition to start the motor and after the temperature gauge shows the needle reading into the yellow, operate the handle marked "Wheels" to the rear position and steer the CC to the takeoff circle.
2. Once inside the takeoff circle, operate the handle marked "Rotor" to the rear and locked position. After locking the steering wheel in place, Use the two handles marked "Up" on either side of the seat to power the CC into the air.
3. In combination with the two handles, use the left and right foot pedals to propel the CC in the desired direction.

Fred's craft was a little one place machine only slightly larger than a compact car with a top speed of eighty mph and a range of only a hundred miles.

The month of May meant the Senior Prom wasn't far away and Teresa and Casey did this prom the same way they did the one last year. Casey grumbled all the way while he rode to school on that old bike with Teresa.

"You know Teresa, I really hate this. I'm going to make you a promise right now. Some day, after we're married, I'm going to give you the biggest, most expensive present there is and a brand new dress to wear when you receive it."

"Don't forget, I told you that I want diamonds and pearls and stacks and stacks of money." Teresa began to giggle and chuckle and Casey caught it and the two of them were laughing so hard at each other, that they had to stop and wait till they were able to continue the rest of the way to school. The prom turned out to be a lot of fun for them after all.

Graduation was a glorious day for all the seniors of SMHS, some more than others. Teresa graduated number one in the senior class with Casey close behind her as number two. Both have won scholarships to colleges, the only way Teresa and Casey could have attended college was with a scholarship.

Teresa will be attending Oklahoma to study to be a Bioagricultural Scientist, and Casey will be attending the University of Colorado to study to be something, but he'll figure it out as he goes. Mitchell graduated thirteenth in the class and was offered a football scholarship at Arizona State.

Chapter 5

The College Years

August 2018

Teresa and Casey were together all summer. They had been participating in the rodeos around the state for five years now and this would be their last. After each rodeo, the two would have dinner and see a movie and enjoy each other's company until they reached their front doors. But it was difficult to go on dates together now because they still had no money and no car. Just those two bicycles and, of course, the two horses of Mr. Castilla that they had been riding.

Their conversation had always been about school and school related activities, but now school was taking them apart. School related activities would be in two different states more than five hundred miles apart. It was a beautiful day in June when Teresa opened her bedroom window and yelled across to Casey.

"It came! Casey! It came!"

"What came, Tease?"

"I've been accepted to Oklahoma, and they sent a whole package of papers, come and see!"

Casey ran next door where Teresa was waiting for him at the front door. She had laid all the contents of the large brown envelope on the dining table and began excitedly talking to her best friend.

"It says that there are about twenty five thousand students in the school at Norman, Oklahoma. Listen to this." Teresa began to read to Casey from the OU brochure.

"The University of Oklahoma was established in 1890, seventeen years before Oklahoma became a state. Today the University is a major national research University that serves the educational, cultural and economic needs of the state region and nation. Located halfway between the Atlantic and Pacific coasts at the boundary between the eastern and western woodlands and the vast western prairie, the University is a gathering place for students and scholars from across the nation and around the globe."

"But I'm no scholar." She said.

"Of course you are. You finished first in the class didn't you? And you took all the hardest classes just to prove to me that you were smarter than I am. And you are."

"There's more, listen to this." She said.

"The University of Oklahoma has eighteen colleges offering a hundred fifty three undergraduate degree programs, a hundred twenty seven masters degree programs, seventy nine doctoral programs, professional degrees in six areas and dual professional and masters programs. OU enrolls more than twenty five thousand students at the Norman campus, and has approximately eighteen hundred fifty faculty members located at three campuses. The University's annual operating budget is over six hundred million dollars. Since the first two degrees in 1898, OU has conferred degrees to more than a hundred eighty thousand individuals. OU is a special place where academic excellence, cultural diversity and a wealth of activities provide opportunities for students to achieve their full potential while making great memories."

"Well you know that I am interested in growing more food in the desert and arid lands and finding ways to feed my people and yours. OU has great agricultural and scientific schools and I applied for the course as a Bioagricultural Scientist."

Teresa was talking but Casey's mind had begun to wander. Teresa has grown into a beautiful woman. She was five feet six inches tall, a hundred and five pounds, black hair, brown eyes, olive skin and a twenty six inch waist, Casey called Tease his "Italian Indian". Casey was lucky to have the love of such a wonderful and smart woman, and he knew it. He was going to miss her and he didn't even know if he had been accepted to a school.

"Casey? Casey! Your mother is here, snap out of it!"

"This came in the mail earlier. I looked for you at home, and you didn't answer, so I came over here. It's from Colorado." Ann said.

The three of them tore into it like kids tearing into a gift on Christmas morning. Each of them grabbed part of the paperwork and Casey got the letter from the school.

"I've been accepted to Colorado! Wow! It says that school starts on the August 25th 2018."

"Hey listen to this."

"At it's first session in 1861, the Territorial Legislature of Colorado passed an act providing for a university at Boulder. The University was formally founded in 1876, the same year that Colorado became the Centennial State. Between 1861 and 1876, Boulder citizens donated land south of town and made gifts from fifteen dollars to a thousand dollars in order to match the fifteen thousand dollars appropriated by the state legislature for construction of the University.

Casey MacKenzie has also grown up, he stands five foot ten inches tall and weighs a hundred eighty pounds with dark brown hair and a flashing smile.

The rest of the summer was filled with laughing and fun for all the members of both families. Teresa would run next door and hug Casey or Ann for no apparent reason and they would laugh together for several minutes after that.

School was scheduled to start soon and the time was fast approaching to board the bus to their schools.

"This is really interesting reading about your school, listen to this." Annika Forsberg, Mitchell's girlfriend began reading the brochure from Arizona State.

"Arizona State University is an internationally recognized university serving approximately fifty thousand students in the Phoenix area. The university provides the highest quality educational experiences to it's students and also sponsors academic, cultural, sports, and social activities throughout the metropolitan area."

"Stop reading that! I don't give a damn about this area, but I must get a degree in something to achieve my goals, and it looks like I'm stuck with this for now. I'll show them how to play football and win and at the same time I'll learn what I need to succeed."

"Mitch honey, I hope you don't get involved with those awful people that you have been hanging around with when you go to school. They scare me." Annie said.

Mitchell never did tell anyone where he went or who he was with all during Junior High and High School, Annie was the only one who knew.

"Why should they scare you, you're one of the Aryan race. You're going to stand by me aren't you?"

Mitchell Cordel was now six feet three inches tall and weighed two hundred pounds and muscular, but he didn't have the training to use all that muscle properly.

Mitchell was a bully all through school. That was what his father taught him. Later in Junior High he met a group of boys who not only agreed with his father's twisted beliefs, but they preached this kind of thinking to him and the other young boys who came their way.

This group of new friends he made back in seventh grade call themselves a "family", thirty years ago they were called a lot of other names, but the closest word to family that was used then was clan.

Mitchell's mind has been corrupted and he doesn't even know it. Pitiful! He has faithfully attended the meetings from the start and has been "promoted" to higher positions of authority and responsibility with each passing year.

The time had come to board the bus for school and go off into the world. Casey and Tease stood together at her bus with lots of good-bye hugs and kisses for each other, but finally the driver told Teresa to get on the bus. Casey's bus was due to leave in an hour, and he stood there in the bus station with a vacant feeling in his gut for that hour. He loved her and now he knew it for sure.

Mitchell didn't have to take the bus. His "family" provided him with a loaner car since the school he will be attending was located right there in Phoenix.

Teresa called Casey about the second week of school. "Hi honey, what are you studying?"

"I've really got some interesting subjects, Introduction to Geology, Petrology, that's the study of rocks and Technical Software."

"I'll be studying agriculture and Attributes of Living Systems, but Logarithmic and Exponential Functions is just too much math for me to handle."

It was only the first semester and Mitchell was complaining about how hard Introduction to Macroeconomics was and how he would rather be playing football. Even though he was very very good on the football field, he won't be the starter this year.

"Hi, Dad. I was just calling to tell you about Christmas break. It starts on the 20th and I have to be back to school on the 20th of January." Casey said.

Fred's new Commutercopter for 2018 was in a showroom in Phoenix last September and he sold all he had on hand and took orders for future delivery. He and his company are working day and night to turn out the orders. The CC was an instant hit with the commuting public and sales went through the roof, at least in Fred's eyes.

One of the first people Fred hired when he began to produce the CC, was Michael MacKenzie. Fred, who was fifty five years old then, took Michael under his wing like a son, and when he mentioned Casey needed a job when he was home from school, Fred said, "Bring him in as soon as he arrives."

Casey worked for Fred during the Christmas break, and Fred asked him back for the summer vacation. It was only minimum wage of four dollars an hour, but it added up fast. Fred had a small production line in a four car garage, and Casey was doing a menial job but Fred took a liking to him and Casey was soaking up everything Fred said like a sponge.

"How'd you like to learn to fly that thing, Casey?

"Wow, you mean it? You bet!" Casey said.

"Let's go."

Fred was one of those guys who was so smart it seemed they never needed to study, they understood everything as soon as they read it. Fred has a BS as an Electronics Engineer and another as an Aeronautical Engineer, and an A & P license. He could build the plane and the motor to propel it and wire it for computers and navigation equipment as well, all from scratch.

The technicians finally got all the stock exchange back up and running two years ago but the banks and mortgage companies and all the other businesses that had failed because of the original stock exchange failure were still out of business, most permanently. But after four years of agonizing financial, emotional and mental anguish, the country was on the road to recovery.

President Scott took this opportunity to address the country on national TV for thirty minutes on March 5th, where he declared the depression officially finished. It was only a matter of weeks that people were being called back to work by some of the companies that weathered the storm. Even though it was still only "Faces and Places", people finally started to have money again. By summer, the recovery was complete. Jobs were available again and the feeling was that everything would soon be back to normal.

The phone rang in Teresa's room as she was studying Biology of Living Organisms. She answered it, "Hello, this is Teresa."

"Hi Tease, are you catching up on your farming math? Ha, ha, ha."

"That's not funny, Casey MacKenzie. Besides taking a heavy load this semester I've been saddled with College Composition too. First math, now English, what's next?"

"I'll trade you. I've got Statistics for Earth Sciences and Introduction to Hydrogeology, not to mention all the other stuff."

Mitchell played football and complained about every class he took. Now that football season was over, he was told by his coach to get down to business with Intermediate Macroeconomics and math.

Casey was looking forward to working for Fred again this summer, but when he returned home on spring break, Fred was packing the place up. "What're you doing Mr. Goss?"

"Since you were here last, I've had some very interesting offers from General Motors, Ford and Chrysler for my little invention here. They offered me so much money and royalties, I couldn't refuse."

"What are you going to do now?"

"I'm moving to a place I have in Colorado far from the cities where I won't be bothered with civilization and I can be alone and enjoy myself. Here's the address, come and see me on one of your breaks from school." Fred said.

The freshman year ended on the eighteenth of May, 2019. Casey and Teresa both found summer jobs back home and both studied everything they could as long as they could study together. The sophomore year will start on the twenty fourth of August and Casey and Teresa were anxious to get started again.

"Teresa my dear, this whole course of study is so interesting. I'm going to take everything I can get in the field of geology and earth sciences. My counselor told me to slow down, he thinks I'm overloaded, but

I can handle it. I've got Planetary Geology, Ocean-ography and math, lots of math."

"Yes, I'm swamped with math too and General Chemistry and Computers in Business too."

Mitchell had moved into the starting quarterback job and was winning games on a regular basis. His foul disposition was thought of as leadership quali-ties by the coaches. Little did they know.

Teresa and Casey spent a lot of time together talk-ing about school and their classes during the break. Christmas time was always something special for the two of them and their families.

"I can't get enough of this stuff, next semester I get to study Coastal Sciences and Earthquakes. I al-ways wanted to know why the earth quakes, I know I quake when I see you, but I know the reason for that."

"Casey you are a mess. You never liked school be-fore and here you are eating it up. I wish you had my courses next semester. I've got Basic Horticulture, which should be pretty easy and Analytic Trigonom-etry. I can't understand why there is so much math." She said.

"That's so you can add up all the ears of corn out in the field on your fingers."

"I hate you, Casey MacKenzie, you smart aleck."

Mitchell was still grumbling about Economics and International Trade, but that was what the course of study his degree was all about.

Casey just had to call Teresa before spring break. He wanted to ask her an important question.

"Would it be OK if I visited you in Oklahoma over spring break?" He said.

"Where would you stay, honey?"

"I thought I could stay with you at your apartment."

"You know that if we do that, that's all we'll do and we both have lots of studying to do. I told you that there will never be anyone else and you will want me to help with the bills because six kids will take a lot of money . . ."

Casey's mind suddenly got stuck on a snag as Tease was talking and he reran those last words over in his mind. "Six kids?" That woke him up. "What did you say?"

"Which part?" She giggled again.

Teresa usually didn't leave school during spring break and this year was no exception. Teresa labored on with such things as Plant Anatomy and Economic Biology, while Casey was singing through twice as many courses and taking electives like Astronomy and Interstellar Astrophysics. Teresa was sure he's crazy or maybe possessed.

Mitchell hates school and hates economics, but he knew he must continue, so he studied, grudgingly. Annika helped him, she did everything for him and kept him at it, but he still complained.

During spring break this year, Casey took Chuck Kinkaid to Fred's place for a week of fun in the Colorado Mountains and a chance to soak up some of the vast knowledge that Fred carries around all day.

Chuck stuck to Fred like glue for the entire week and the two of them talked about astrophysics and space travel. Casey went flying into the beautiful mountains almost every day. Some days he spotted deer and other animals, some days he didn't see a thing.

School was out for the year on the seventeenth of May 2020. It was a long year.

Casey worked and saved all the money he made from his jobs during Christmas vacation, summer vacation and Christmas vacation the next year to buy the ring for her. "I bought something for you."

At four dollars per hour forty hours a week, after taxes it came to just over two thousand dollars. The ring wasn't much, just a little one third carat on a real gold band, but it was a steal at nineteen ninety five.

"Will you marry me?" He opened the box and handed it to her.

"It's beautiful and yes, I will, but not now."

"When?" He asked.

"Ask me again next year." She put the ring back into the box and handed it back to Casey.

"But, Tease!"

"I'm just living up to the name you gave me, honey." She grinned at him and stuck her finger under her chin and batted her eyes at him.

This year when school started in August 2020 it would be their Junior year in school. Teresa continued her agricultural courses with Introductory Soil Science and Professional Writing, and Casey had Probability and Statistics and Physics of the Solid Earth.

Mitchell was complaining that everywhere he turned his courses had the economics word in it. One thing you can't take away from Mitchell though, he was good on the football field. Arizona State finally found a couple of receivers and Mitchell led the team to a twelve and one season and a berth in the Rose Bowl. They lost to a far superior Oklahoma team by the score of 28 to 7. But Mitchell would be back, he guaranteed it.

After a long campaign toward the election on the second of November 2020, President Greg Scott was re-elected for a second term. President Scott promised better times, more jobs and a time of prosperity.

Later that month NASA placed a call to the Oval Office.

"Mr. President, we have found that blue planet on our star maps. What would you like for us to do?

"I think there should be no press at this time. Let's just keep it to ourselves for now. We don't know enough right now to talk about this revelation. Now is the time to find out all we can about this planet, especially how far away it is from earth."

Teresa and Casey celebrated their twenty first birthdays together at home with friends and family on the tenth of January during Christmas break. In less than two weeks, they would be back to the grind with such courses as Feed Formulation and Calculus for Biological Scientists, and Mapping and Technical Graphics and Quantum Mechanics and Magnetism.

Bruce Gardner was a friend and classmate of Teresa's and they studied together sometimes. She had told him all about the love of her life and he had done the same. Bruce was reading the newspaper when she entered the classroom and sat next to him.

"Hey, Teresa. I see where a guy I know made front page news, listen to this."

"Hermann Rolf Kuhlmann, Coolie for short, an inventor, forty five years old with a Masters degree in Physics and a Ph.D. in Astrophysics and worked twenty six years in the field of astrophysical sciences has offered to unveil his latest invention for the US Government. His invention, named Roamer, was not his first, but it is his most important invention, and is a way to prove how to move a particle faster than light."

Casey is trying to catch up on some of the extra classes he was taking. It was hard to imagine someone wanting to study Analytical Mechanics and the Geological Record of Life just for fun.

Casey and Chuck Kinkaid visited Fred again during spring break in March. Casey was finally beginning to hold his own during the super technical discussions, but neither of them ever questioned his ability to fly that old army helicopter. Every time Casey flew it, he got better.

School was finished for the year again in May, and Casey was eager to see Teresa and spend three long hot months with her again.

"Teresa, when are you going to say yes to my question?"

"What is your question, smart guy?"

"Will you marry me?"

"Oh, OK. If you insist." She giggled every time she heard the question.

"When?" He asked.

"Next summer. After we graduate."

"Would you please accept this then, I've been carrying it around for a long time trying to give it to you." He said.

"Casey honey, I accepted your proposal of marriage that day when we were thirteen, don't you remember? Why have you been worried?"

She hugged and kissed him and he turned into a bowl of jelly right there in her arms. As soon as Casey left, Marie and her daughter were yelling and jumping around the house for hours.

"Mom! You're not supposed to be eves dropping when Casey is pouring his heart out to me."

"Yes dear. I was worried that you were going to make him wait again. Did you set the date yet?" Mom asked.

"Yes, July 30th after we graduate."

"I'll take care of everything here at home, but I'll need money for the cake and some of the other stuff." Marie said.

"Just one more question Teresa honey, why did you make him wait so long?" Mom asked.

Their Senior year will start on the twenty second of August. Only one more year to go. Teresa was back to the books with Livestock Practicums and

Casey was pouring over Oceanography and Theoretical Mechanics.

Mitchell's feelings haven't changed.

"The only good thing about Economics is that it is 'The study of Money'."

Mitchell was the quarterback for Arizona State and they again won a berth at the Rose Bowl, but this game ended differently from the game last year, Mitchell threw everything but the kitchen sink at the opposition. His receivers and backs caught every pass he threw and ran right through their line like it wasn't even there. Arizona State won the National Championship which put Mitchell squarely where he most wanted to be, in the limelight.

No one at Arizona State knew or caught him at it, but Mitchell cheated regularly in all his classes to get through school. Every time there was something said about Mitchell related to any impropriety, he blamed it on someone else and never did get caught. Another trait he learned from his father.

The scholastic load on a senior is a big one to start with, add to that the impending marriage and career after graduation, and it adds up to a long tough year for both of them.

"Hello Teresa. I reserved the church for the wedding and the reception after. Reverend Stanley said he would be happy to perform the ceremony."

In September, the CommuterCopter was refined and finally built and marketed by the big three auto companies. Fred retained a royalty from his sale of the patent and drawings of it.

"But one big problem that no one has given the slightest thought to is, there are no "air streets", no laws by states, cities or towns, no speed limits, no nothing. People could get killed." Fred said.

"Good evening. This is World News Tonight for October 4th, 2021. An earthquake of seven point oh shook the area known as Alajuela near a little town of Arenal, Costa Rica. No one was killed but nearly all of the houses and buildings in the town were leveled."

Maria waited patiently for Teresa to come home on Christmas break so that she can pick out her dress. The two of them spent all day at one dress shop until Tease finally found the one she liked.

Teresa studied Translocation in Plants, and Casey was still carrying a big load with General Astronomy and Stratigraphic Sciences. He seems to be fascinated with both the earth and the stars, but didn't know which he found more interesting.

Mitchell had stopped complaining about school since he was the big star of the Rose Bowl and everyone at the school had been bedazzled with him.

The airways were becoming more crowded and therefore accidents on the airways were increasing and on the highways were decreasing. The main problem with the CC was when two CC's collide with each other, both aircraft were thrown out of control and both plummet to earth, killing the occupants, one hundred percent of all CC accidents were fatal to all involved.

The Federal Government in their infinite wisdom said that the sudden increase in deaths in the Commutercopter was because of a lack of training on the part of the pilots or drivers, and they made classes mandatory prior to sale or licensing. The actual problem was two fold, first there were no air streets, no state federal or local laws and no speed limits; second, the car companies made it a lot cheaper than Fred's model. The big companies were using cheaper materials in all the components, the parts break easier, engine mounts break, and passengers die.

"Your sister Linda said she would be your Maid of Honor and her daughter would carry the rings."

Teresa stayed in her room at school during spring break again. She had Botany and Molecular and General Genetics coming up this semester and she thought she needed to study for it. Casey on the other hand was sailing along toward graduation and had no worries about courses like Planetary Sciences, The Planets, Moon and Rings.

"I got a good deal on the cake from Mrs. Trujillo at the cake shop. She was so happy that you and Casey are getting married."

School was out on the fifteenth of May, 2022 and the graduation was held on the May nineteenth. Teresa graduated at the top of her class and earned her BA as a Bioagricultural Scientist. Casey earned a BS in GeoPhysics and all the extra work filled out a Masters in Planetary Sciences. Mitchell, notwithstanding his excellent performance on the football field, graduated last in his class with a BA in Economics.

"I'm getting married in the morning." He was singing the words.

Casey was bouncing around the house all day singing that old song out of tune and worst of all, he doesn't know any of the words except the opening six words.

July 30 2022, the wedding is today.

Chapter 6

Flavio Archuletta

July 30 2022

"Teresa Basilio, do you take this man to be your lawfully wedded husband - - ?"

"I do."

"Casey MacKenzie, do you take this woman to be your lawfully wedded wife?"

"I do."

It was a beautiful wedding for a pair of poor kids from the wrong side of the tracks, and now they're on their way to a new job and a chance for a new life. Casey and Teresa MacKenzie stayed over night at the Ramada Inn and packed the 1983 Dodge pickup with everything they owned and started on their magic move to Carson City.

Casey didn't have much money and they needed a car to get to Nevada so Tease could go to work. His dad knew a guy with an old truck that had been parked in his back yard for years and talked him into selling it to Casey for fifty dollars. He and his dad spent some time and another three hundred dollars to get it roadworthy. It's not much and it's almost forty years old too, but when you're broke you take what you can get.

On the drive across Arizona and Nevada, both of them had plenty of chances to look at the countryside and talk about all the things they had done during the time they spent in school and what they planned to do in the future.

"I met the nicest guy at school. His name is Bruce Gardner and he has that same blonde hair as that awful Mitchell had, but Bruce is a real gentleman. He is smart and he cares about other people too. He was studying to be a Space Systems Engineer and we had some classes together."

Casey told her about Chuck and how the two of them visited Fred and flew his old helicopter again. Fred really took to Chuck and the two of them talked about technical stuff the whole time during their visit.

"Remember when we saw that yellow haze in the sky? It looks like the sky is doing it again. See there." Teresa said and pointed to the yellow haze they had seen hanging over the horizon to the south for the past several months.

"I'm really happy about this job, Casey. The State of Nevada has a new program to reclaim the desert there and grow crops on the land. It sounds so exciting and that's been my dream all along."

Highway 395, the road up from the southern part of the state joins Highway 50 just outside of Carson City and becomes Carson Street. Casey was happy that the long hot drive was over and was looking for a cheap motel with air conditioning to hole up in, but Tease has other ideas.

"Look Casey, Paloverde Street. Turn here! Quick!"

It was only a few blocks before she saw the "For Rent" sign in the yard.

"There! Stop there!"

She almost jumped out of the truck before it stopped moving, and ran up the front steps to the porch and through the open front door.

Casey parked in front and by the time he entered the house, he could hear Tease talking a mile a minute, as she usually does when she was excited. The first words he heard her speak clearly were, "We'll take it!"

Casey found her talking animatedly with a woman in a blue dress with a name tag on her left shoulder that said "Betty". Betty was a real estate agent who represented several landlords around town and she had just stopped by to check the house after the last tenants had moved out over the weekend.

"Isn't it wonderful? My first house! I'm so excited."

Of course, Casey would never have guessed that she was excited, she was bouncing around the room like a rubber ball. Tease held up the key for Casey to see, then she introduced Casey as her loving husband and Betty took them both through the house.

It was a wood frame house that was at least seventy or eighty years old with a nice new two color green paint scheme. It was only a one story bungalow of about a thousand square feet with two bedrooms and two baths and a basement, but it had the charm that Teresa wanted. There is a one car garage in back on the alley. It has carpet in most of the rooms, but is completely unfurnished except for the stove.

"It's OK I guess. How much?" He asked.

"Only eight hundred."

"A month? For this?"

"We need to get some furniture." She said.

"Do we have any money?"

"A little." He said.

The next day was consumed with shopping trips to used furniture stores looking for bargains and just plain cheap stuff. They bought a refrigerator, a bed, one couch and a kitchen table and chairs before the money ran out.

During the week prior to Teresa's first day with the State of Nevada, five Mexican Generals were following the orders given them by the President of Mexico, Flavio Archuletta. These five generals were massing their troops in five strategically picked locations along the border on the Mexican side, Nuevo Laredo, Ciudad Acuna, Ciudad Juarez, Nogales and Tijuana.

Flavio had become more and more angry over the past several months, with a cold and sneezing continually. Finally he snapped and decided to take back all the land the US had stolen from Mexico over the centuries past. He has been fed bad information from his advisors and his military generals. For some reason, the whole country seems to be mad at the whole world and the US is closest and easiest to be mad at.

In accordance with the orders of the President, all five generals had a meeting before the attack with all their officers to give them instructions and specific directions. All written out and given to the Generals by the President himself.

"Colonels, each of you will command a Brigade of men and you will capture and secure the military bases. If there is more than one base, you will secure the first and use their equipment to transport

your men to the next base and follow the same pro-
cedures. Once this is accomplished, you will fan out
over half the distance to the predesignated points on
these maps to meet your amigos."

"You Majors are to take all Federal and State
buildings and secure them as I have instructed you.
Each of you Captains are to take a squad of men
to each and every police and sheriff's station, take
and secure them as I have said. This list contains the
addresses of all the police stations, sheriff's offices,
State and Federal buildings in our target area."

"All teams are to be on station at exactly ten hundred hours next Wednesday morning. Until then
each of you must practice the exercise until each man
under your command knows exactly what he must
do. Dismissed!"

Monday August 7

Teresa's first day of work for the State of Nevada was
very exciting for her. She left for work a half hour
early so that she could be on time. She walked into
the front entry foyer and up to the reception desk.

"Hi! I'm Teresa MacKenzie and this is my first day
working here. Can you tell me where the Department
of Agriculture is?"

"Up the stairs to the second floor, turn left and
three doors down on the left."

She dutifully climbed the steps and found the correct office door. When she entered the girl was expecting her, the receptionist must have called ahead.
The secretary introduced Teresa around the office
and her new boss took Teresa to the Human Relations Office to be processed in as a new hire.

Teresa was as high as a cloud for the rest of the day. Everyone she met seemed so friendly to her and helpful. When quitting time came, they had to tell her to go home, she was so engrossed into the information they had given her.

Tuesday August 8

Tuesday morning Teresa dragged Casey with her to work to meet her boss and some of the others. Casey was very uncomfortable with all of this until he shook a man's hand who said, "How nice to meet you Casey. I'm Leonard Wilhelm. I work here with your wife and these other people, come and let me introduce you to some of my friends."

Leonard walked Casey down the hall to the big double doors and they entered the Senate Chamber. "Casey, this is State Senator Williams and this is the room where we meet and do our work."

Just then a young man came up to the three of them and said, "Excuse me Governor, but I have a call waiting for you in your office."

"Well, duty calls. It was nice talking to you and you must come and see me sometime when we can spend more time together, Casey."

Casey stood there for several minutes with his mouth open and nothing coming out.

Wednesday August 9

Wednesday morning came and the five armies moved with practiced precision as they simultaneously crossed the border into the US. Each of the armies were commanded by an Army General. The First Army by General Orlando Garcia, the Second Army by General Hector Padilla, the Third Army by General Arturo Trujillo, the Fourth Army by General Andres Valdez, and the Fifth Army by General Diego Valenzuela.

By four p.m. each team had secured their objective and the Mexican Armed Forces had captured the US-Mexican border from the Gulf of Mexico to the Pacific Ocean.

When the news of the invasion was received in Washington, panic stirred in the halls of the Pentagon and the White House.

The Mexican Armies continued to move toward the tiny border towns like ants moving across the land toward a picnic meal.

"Casey! Come quick! Listen!" She shouted and Casey came running.

"Good evening. This is World News Tonight for August 9th, 2022. Mexico has invaded cities, towns and military bases in Texas, New Mexico, Arizona and California and captured the United States-Mexican border from the Gulf of Mexico to the Pacific Ocean. At this time, all Federal and State buildings as well as all local police and fire facilities have been captured and are now under Mexican control. White House and Pentagon spokesmen have not been able to be reached for comment."

"I'm really worried about this. Both of our families are down there. What if the Mexicans capture Phoenix? I wonder if they are hurting anyone. I'm going to call my mother to see if she's OK. I'll ask about your mom and dad too." Teresa said.

Tease was on the phone as soon as the television news about the invasion was over.

Thursday August 10

President Scott held a televised press conference early the next morning where he declared war on Mexico. Casey wrestled with what he should do about the war all day and when Tease came home from work she told him to join the service if he wanted to.

"Go ahead, I'll be alright here." She said.

Casey agreed. "Maybe I can help stop the war sooner."

Tease was the best thing that had ever happened to Casey, but he couldn't turn his back on the fact that this war was in their backyard and he had an obligation to help if he could. Besides, Fred had taught him to fly that old Army surplus helicopter Fred had behind the CC plant back home. He called it a funny name, "Huey something". Besides he had just finished school at Colorado, maybe they could use him somewhere.

Friday August 11

The first thing Friday morning, Casey went bouncing into the US Air Force recruiter's office.

"Hi, I want to join. I've been to school and I can fly a helicopter and I'd like to fly them and learn to fly a fighter plane in the war."

"Sorry kid, we don't have helos, we only fly fighters, the best fighters in the world, I might add."

Casey was undaunted by his rejection by the Air Force and he walked across the street to the Post Office where he found the Army recruiter and presented him with the same request.

"Sorry kid, we don't have any fighters only helicopters. I can guarantee you helicopter school for thirty eight weeks at Fort Rucker, Alabama. You'll probably get about eight weeks shaved off because of your prior experience. When you graduate you'll be a Second Lieutenant in the US Army. Then you could go for pilot training on trainers and administrative fixed wing planes. After pilot training school, you might even come out a First Lieutenant, it's only an additional twelve to fourteen weeks."

"But I want to fly a fighter plane and be in combat."

Only one stop left for Casey and that was the Navy down the hall.

"We would love to have you, we have helos and all the fighters you want. The Air Force say theirs are the best, but look at these photos on the wall here, and you can fly off a carrier too. When did you want to enlist?"

"Would now be too soon?" He said.

"You will go in at grade E5 until you are commissioned in Officers Candidate School. It is thirteen weeks at Pensacola Naval Air Station, then you will come out as an Ensign. After a weekend pass, you will spend eighteen months in flight school at Pensacola. Let's see, you should be graduating about March of '24."

It took Casey the rest of the day to round up everything. His birth certificate, high school diploma, marriage license and the diploma and all the papers from CU, but he finally did it and was sworn in at three in the afternoon. He walked home singing all the way, "You're in the Navy now." He caught a flight that weekend to Florida and he was off and running.

Mitchell graduated from Arizona State in May, the same as Casey and Teresa, but when the war started in August, he signed up for Law school the same day.

"I'm not going into any war. If I want a war, I'll start one of my own."

While Casey was in basic training, Tease had been writing letters to Casey often about her job and some of the interesting things going on in their new home.

"You'll never believe this, but there were real live camel races over in Virginia City this weekend. I sure was tired after I got home. I ran in the 'Dirty Dusty Damn Hot Relay', that's the real name honest, Saturday. I did the Five K run and boy was I beat after that. I'm going to see a doctor Monday, I've been really tired lately."

Casey read the letters over and over, it gave him a good feeling to know Tease was safe.

October 22

He opened the letter and there in big letters she had written, "It's a boy!!"

Her letter continued, "No, not really, I won't know for sure for three or four more months, but I sure hope it is. It looks like you're going to be a daddy soon."

She went on to say that she had been feeling bad and went to a new doctor there in town and found she was pregnant.

"Doctor Ellis said it is due in April. I hope you like the name Sean."

Casey went through the next seven weeks of OCS like he was Superman. All he could think of was that his own beautiful Italian Indian wife was going to have his baby and he had a weekend pass coming as soon as this course was over.

The November weekend Casey spent at home with Tease was pure heaven. He was an officer in the US Navy and he was going to get to fly helicopters and a jet fighter too. Teresa was so beautiful and she was going to have a baby. His baby! He couldn't stop hugging her, but all too soon it was time to go back to the real world and that meant back to Florida and the Navy school.

Casey put his mind to school like he had never done before. Whatever was asked of him, he gave double. He studied the books, he practiced in the trainers. He flew every plane they had, over and over and over.

It only took one semester for Mitchell to realize that Law was the right field for him.

"I didn't realize how much I liked this. This is my ticket to money, fame and power."

The US was not going to stand by and allow the Mexican government to continue with its insane ways. US forces invaded Mexico from all directions!

They landed troops on the beaches on both sides of the Gulf of California and took Baja California without even a shot being fired. The same thing happened in the peninsula of Yucatan.

In both places they took thousands and thousands of prisoners, most of them went willingly. The Colonel in charge of the forces in the Baja sent an urgent message to Washington.

"What do we do with all these people?"

"Colonel, I have a reply to your urgent query to Washington, sir."

"Go ahead and read it, Major."

"All who do not speak English are to be put in prison camps. Those who do, will be used as conscript workers in the prison camps and other places. You will find whole cities and towns to be turned into prison camps with a battalion of troops guarding them and will funnel all prisoners into these camps."

"Major, this reply sounds like something I read about in the history books. Take two helicopters and a squad of your men and go find a suitable place to house these prisoners. Then contact the Army Engineers to build the necessary fences around the town you pick and transport all the prisoners to that town. Be sure to provide all the necessary food and water and do not! I repeat! Do not! Kill even one of the prisoners. Or there will be hell to pay, and my name will be 'Hell'! Dismissed!"

It wasn't long before the Colonel had another disturbing message to be sent to Washington.

"The longer we stay here, the worse my men get. They are becoming more irritated with each day.

Every man in the command is sick and tired. Most are sneezing almost uncontrollably. Something is wrong here."

The cloud can be seen in the distance moving east through the Caribbean over the islands.

April of '23 was a very special time, Casey knew that the time was short. He would talk to Tease as often as possible and she kept him informed of her progress. Casey wanted to be there when his son was born.

"Ensign MacKenzie reporting, Sir."

"Yes, what is it Mr. MacKenzie?"

"Request permission to return home to witness the birth of my son, Sir." He said.

"Request granted. You may have three days leave from the time your plane lands in Carson City until it leaves again, now get going, time is running out, Mister."

Casey immediately ran for the phone to call the airline and more importantly, to call Tease.

"Hold on for a few days, I'll be there."

It was only a short time after the beginning of the war that Cuba came to the aid of Mexico. Cuba mobilized all of their three hundred thousand military members and dispatched a third of them to Mexico to fight against the Imperialist dogs of the north.

It was a long, long year in '23, but soon it would be time to graduate from flight school and fly the real thing. Casey hadn't seen his son since he was born and he missed his beloved Tease, but someone had to stop the war and Casey thought he would be the one to do it. He hoped he was good enough to get stationed somewhere near the fighting.

This is an election year, and President Scott is completing his second term and must step down for the newly elected President, Charles Cummings.

Casey graduated from pilot training first in his class. He was given his choice of assignments and picked the biggest carrier in the Caribbean, the Enterprise, and placed himself right into battle.

The Dominican Republic and Haiti joined Mexico and Cuba in the war against the US the day after Casey reported on board. The Island Nations Forces came into Mexico behind the US forces already on land and surprised them at their back. Fierce fighting in the thick green forests of the Yucatan followed. Many casualties on both sides were a result of this action.

During the rest of that year and into the following year, Casey distinguished himself as a pilot. He shot down twenty nine enemy planes, disabled enemy ships and provided ground cover for LST's on the coast of Mexico.

One of the most unusual feats that he performed was over Cuba. While returning from a patrol of the Caribbean Islands with his team mates, he saw a SAM fired from a battery on the island of Cuba.

Casey was a good pilot and he knew it, but when he flew toward the heat-seeker and it turned around and began to chase him, he was wondering if he had finally gotten in over his head. The SAM chased him in a power dive toward the ground and the missile battery, where he pulled the stick with all his might and leveled off over the water.

Once the battery was silenced, he unloaded all four of his missiles into the munitions storage bunkers where the SAMs were stored. It looked like the explosion made a crater a hundred feet across and at least fifty feet deep, but Casey wasn't staying around to watch.

The very next day, his team was on the same patrol when he saw an ICBM rise from the launching pad. It only took a second to identify it as an old Russian-made SS-462C ICBM fired at the US. He attacked the huge missile with all the firepower he could muster and knocked it out of the sky.

He nearly knocked himself out of the sky too. The blast was seen from his ship a thousand miles away. Fortunately the warhead dropped into the water in the Bermuda Triangle and he wasn't going after it, no matter what. Cuba suddenly became the focus of attention of the Caribbean fleet and was soon overwhelmed by the superior air and sea power of the American forces.

After Casey was finished being stupid in the air over Cuba, he found more letters and pictures from Teresa and his son Sean waiting for him back aboard ship. Casey may be tough and a brilliant pilot, but one look at the photos of that baby brings tears to his eyes every time.

Hermann Rolf Kuhlmann, called Coolie by his friends, has finished his design on Spector. He put in a call to the US government to present his design and explain what he has done. It was a short meeting with Government officials. They were not interested in any new technology unless it is involved with weapons of war.

But there was one man in attendance at the meeting, who was very impressed with Coolie and his invention, Bruce Gardner, a young NASA Space Systems Engineer. Bruce recognized the application of the design immediately and phoned his supervisor with a glowing report on Coolie and Spector.

"See if you can interview him in private in his home as soon as possible. Have Kinkaid assist you with this project. Report to me as soon as you return." He was told.

Bruce talked to Coolie and they made an appointment to visit him in his home the next week for more information on his new project.

Hermann Kuhlmann lived in a little town outside Bemidji, Minnesota called Redlake. Not a crossroads for two young engineers from NASA who were looking for a personal visit and interview with one of the foremost scientists and inventors in the world.

But travel they must, to Redlake for this very special time in their life. It was white everywhere when the plane landed in Minneapolis and seemed to get whiter as they drove north to their destination.

"Dr. Kuhlmann, would you explain this new invention a little more for us please."

"As you two may remember, I showed a new design a few years ago that I called Roamer. Its primary purpose was to move a particle faster than light. I believe with that design I can move a spacecraft through space faster than light."

The two young engineers were fascinated with every word.

"I believe Spector will afford me the opportunity to move that same spacecraft through time."

Both of them were aghast.

"Through time? Is that even possible?"

"Yes! There are many bugs to be worked out, but it does work. Would you like a demonstration?"

"Would we ever!"

The three of them went to the workshop in back of the garage for the demonstration. There were many black marks on the floor which looked like paint which was spilled.

"You must use a lot of black paint, sir."

"No, no. The device emits a very powerful light as it operates, the greater the setting, the more light. When the device is pointed toward an object and operated, the light will etch an outline of the object, a shadow, on the ground or other solid object. That is the black marks you see here on the floor."

They carefully put everything in the exact places and adjusted the device for ten minutes into the future.

"These are welding goggles. Put them on so you won't damage you eyes from the light."

With everything in place and set, Coolie operated the device.

FLASH!

A blinding flash of light filled the room and the little wooden stool was gone, but it's shadow remained, painted on the floor. The three of them sat there in their chairs watching the spot where the stool had been and watching their wristwatches intently.

In exactly ten minutes and nine seconds, the little wooden stool suddenly reappeared before their eyes.

The war was finally over in the spring of '25 and everyone on board the ship heaved a sigh of relief. Casey was decorated with the Distinguished Flying Cross and the Silver Star for his actions in the war.

"Casey, I'm very proud to have presented these medals to you for your exemplary actions, and this part of my job is one of the very best. It is my honor to promote you to Lieutenant and pin these bars on your shoulder." All hands cheered and applauded for him.

As soon as the ceremony was over and some of the pilots were standing around, one of them asked in a loud voice, "How many enemy kills does it take to be an ace?"

The reply came also in a loud voice, "It don't matter, he got twenty nine of them and that's enough." Everyone on the flight deck laughed and congratulated Casey.

The war with Mexico and the Caribbean islands ended in May, only a few days before Mitchell graduated from Arizona's Law School. Law school was no different than any of the other schools he attended. He learned long ago how to cheat and get away with it. And if he was caught, how to place the blame on another student and swear to it.

May of '25 was a very full month, Mitchell graduated then married Annika and he was only out of
school for a short two week vacation, when he was
offered a job with a big law firm in Phoenix after he
passed the Bar Exam.

He knew he must do menial work at the law firm
for a long time, but he also knew this was another
chance for him to use all the skills and talents he
knows best, lying, cheating and stealing. A sure way
for him to endear himself to the bosses, and finally
he would get the case to make his name.

As a final consideration of the surrender after the
war, US Navy ships surround each of the Caribbean
islands and forcibly removed the present governments and installed US representative governments.

Chapter 7

Annexation

June 2025

Annexation can be traumatic or it can be a happy event. For Mexico it was traumatic for the President, the Military and all the politicians, but very happy for the people. The people didn't want a war with anyone in the first place, but least of all with their friends and neighbors of the United States.

The first order of business was to apportion the country of Mexico into manageable sized states and incorporate those states into the United States of America. This became the job of the Department of the Interior personnel to explain this procedure to both countries, and who better to give the speech of explanation, than the Secretary of the Interior himself. The press conference was held in Mexico City before all the cameras and microphones from both interested countries media.

The Secretary seemed calm and self-assured as he faced the cameras.

"Mexico will be divided into four separate states. The first of these will be Yucatan. Its northern border will cut across the country at the ninety fifth meridian which will give us the first state of Mexico and the fifty first state in these United States. The temporary capital of this state will be Campeche until a new capital city can be built at the innermost point along the bay where the Candelatia River meets the Caribbean Sea."

"Moving in a northerly direction, the next border will cut across the country at the twenty sixth parallel, leaving the state of Lower Mexico below this line. It will become the fifty second state of the United States. Mexico City will be the capital of this state."

"The third state will be defined when we continue the southern border of Arizona straight across the countryside to the Gulf of California. In this way we have made the state of Upper Mexico the fifty-third state with Monterrey as the state capital. This change in the southern border of Arizona will give Arizona an outlet onto the oceans of the world. We are making immediate plans for a new city to be built in Arizona which will be a seaport on the Gulf of California."

"The fourth and last state will be defined when the border of California is realigned. From the point where the southern border of California meets the Pacific, we will draw a diagonal line toward the Gulf of California to the point where the Colorado River empties into the gulf. This line will be the new southern border of California. The river will divide the two states of California and Arizona, and all below the California border will be the fourth state of Mexico, Pacifica, and the fifty-fourth state of the United States. A new capital city, to be named Peace, will be built at the Bay of Peace."

"Puerto Rico will be the fifty-fifth state. Haiti and the Dominican Republic have been consolidated into one state, named Columbus, with one Governor and Legislature as the fifty-sixth state. Jamaica will be the fifty-seventh state and Cuba the fifty-eighth." He said.

The combination of Mexican, American and Cuban forces took its toll on the countryside of Mexico. There would be much reconstruction needed of capital and legislative buildings in Mexico City and around the country. The most pressing matter of reconstruction was transportation. All roads and rail lines were severely damaged. Governors and their staff personnel must be appointed and housed in the four capital cities of the newly formed states.

In order to establish each new state, priority lists were being made and personnel were being contacted and confirmed from all around the country to fill the many staff positions that were needed. Construction of normal everyday housing, schools and safety buildings will be a very high priority among the occupation forces.

Each state would need in addition to the military occupation force, a Governor, Deputy Governor, five State Senators and five State Representatives and one Military Liaison. All of these people will be brought in from the "Upper 48" to fill the positions and get the job done.

Keeping the peace and installing the new governments in the Caribbean area was fabulous duty and great weather, and Casey was loving it. No more dodging missiles and enemy fighters who wanted to put him into Davy Jones Locker. The ships of the Caribbean Fleet periodically would call in at all the ports along the American coast, the islands and the coast of South America. One of the best was Port au Prince in the new state of Columbus.

The Secretary's speech was found to be very fascinating by many members of the crew of the Enterprise. Many of them were from western states and understood what the changes would mean.

Casey mused to himself, "I wonder if this ship could anchor in the Gulf off shore from Arizona City? I could fly home in ten minutes."

Bruce and Chuck have been detailed by NASA to work with Coolie and report on whatever progress they might have. After two months of eighteen hour days and nights, they decided to go back to NASA for a rest and for all three of them to collect their thoughts regarding the problems they were stumbling upon.

After a weekend of nothing but sleep and mental rest, Bruce and Chuck reported to Roger Pond's office.

"Come in. Sit down. Have something to drink, non-alcoholic of course, and tell me what you have. The waiting has been eating away at me ever since you first called me from Washington."

Bruce and Chuck started to talk at the same time.

"Go ahead." Chuck said.

"Roger, Dr. Kuhlmann has the most inventive time travel device I have ever seen, or even imagined." Bruce said.

"It can send an item into the future or the past, we think, depending on the various settings and adjustments made during preparation of the device." Chuck said.

"There is no physical movement of the item which is sent through time. I mean if we sent this chair here in the middle of the room forward in time, it would disappear from our view until it physically returned into our time stream and reappeared in the exact same spot as we see it now." Bruce said.

"What good is this to us? How can we use it? Does Kuhlmann have some ideas or plans to make it work for space travel and what we are doing?" Roger asked.

"You remember that thing he called Roamer, don't you? If we can couple the two of these together, this device can send us back in time and Roamer can make us move at the speed of light, we can travel through time and space at the same time. Wouldn't that be worth something?" Bruce said.

"Alright, from this day forward, you two are detailed to Dr. Kuhlmann for the duration of the time to complete the research and build a prototype of his newest device and bring it here to me. Now get going. And keep me posted!" Roger said.

It was a long trip back to Redlake in the spring, when the temperature in Houston was already into the seventies and when their plane landed there was white still to be seen in patches with the temperature hovering in the middle thirties.

Bruce, Chuck and Coolie worked on Spector day and night with tiny glimmers of hope coming off and on. The spring dragged into the summer and into autumn with the leaves turning colors and falling to the ground.

But when the first snow began to fall in Redlake all three of them had to stop. January first 2027 was not the celebration they had planned. The three of them celebrated with pizza and beer and not many smiles.

"We've been here all year and haven't got it yet." Bruce said.

Winter turned into spring with three major breaks. They tested it on a dog and the dog came through it alive. The biggest break up to that time.

"We must test this on a person. Who wants to volunteer?" Coolie asked.

"Not me."

"Not me."

"Come on, I'd do it but I'm the smart one." Coolie laughed at his joke and both Bruce and Chuck joined in.

"How long should we send the subject away?" Chuck asked.

"It should be a good test, an hour?" Coolie said.

"Do you think we could pay someone to do this?" Bruce asked.

"Yeah, let's go to town and pay someone, I don't want to be the first one to get zapped." Chuck asked.

Their fears overcame them and they went to town to find someone who help them with their experiment. It took an offer of five hundred dollars for Yvonne Archer to agree to go with them.

For that much money, Yvonne was happy to do anything they wanted. The two younger ones were kind of cute and she might just enjoy this "experiment" they asked her to do with them.

Yvonne sat on the little stool while the three of them readied the equipment and paid no attention to her.

"Are you ready, miss?" Coolie asked.

"I - uh - yes. You want to do it here?" She asked.

"Let me explain what we are going to do." Coolie explained in great detail what they thought the device would do, and that they wanted her to observe everything that happened while she was on this little one hour trip. Take this pen and pad and write whatever you see.

The equipment was ready and the test began.

FLASH!

She disappeared before their eyes and the clock was started. The chair didn't disappear, just the woman. The three of them stood there dumbfounded.

"There must be an adjustment made if the object is living tissue or not, I adjusted it to the setting for the dog. We can send the person sitting on a chair but not the chair, or we can send the chair but not the person. This is a real problem." Coolie said.

It was exactly one hour and three seconds that Yvonne appeared standing next to the stool in the middle of the room. The flood of questions from the three men must have been overwhelming to her.

"That wasn't very funny. First you blinded me with that light, then you took the stool away and I've been standing here for a long time and my legs hurt now. Don't you guys have a comfortable place to sit in this house?" She said.

"What did you see when you stood there? Tell me everything." Coolie was almost drooling as he asked her.

"Here. I wrote something. I can't remember anything though."

Yvonne had no memory of the time between the two events, she knew that she had been sitting and the stool disappeared and she fell on the floor, but that was all.

"She has written that she stood in the middle of the room, but she was alone. We were not there with her and the stool was not there, but the house and all its contents were. How is this possible?" Coolie asked.

Bruce, Chuck and Coolie were finally convinced that the design was complete. There were still problems to solve, but that would come with time and experience.

"In order for us to travel in time and space, we must remember why we are there when we get to the place we are going so that we can get back to where we started, which is here on earth. When we are moving backward in time and our knowledge is in the here and now, we must make a device to remind us of our mission." Coolie said.

"We need an electrical engineer to design and build this memory module for us, who can we get for the job?" Bruce asked.

They decided to call Roger and put the monkey on his back. It was only two weeks later that Bruce answered the door and found a young man holding an envelope standing there.

"This is to introduce Ken Hiroshi. He is the smartest Electrical Engineer NASA has and will surprise you. He speaks, writes and understands Japanese, Chinese, Korean, English and at least four other languages, so be on your toes. Love Roger."

Things happened very quickly after Ken's arrival into the Minnesota Maniacs Club. Within only a few more weeks the design was complete and a good solid memory module was designed and built. It was time to go back to the NASA office in Houston where it was warm and do a demo for Roger Pond with a human subject. Roger had previously selected the subject.

Once in the NASA offices, the three of them all began to talk and try to explain the amazing properties of their experiments. Two men were detailed to find a test subject and bring him to the office. The meeting went on for hours. Coolie explained in great detail the test they wanted to perform. The man agreed because of the huge sum of money they promised him.

Their equipment was set up in the office and the four of them put on the welding glasses and Coolie operated the controls.

FLASH!

There always seems to be a little rat snooping around, and this was no exception. Peeping through the door from the hall was Delmer. Delmer saw the flash and the man disappear, nothing more, but that was enough for him. He ran out of there immediately.

For some unknown reason, Roger's subject was angry at the beginning of the test and calm at the end. Coolie examined the shadow while the others talked to the man.

"This shadow looks different from the others I've seen. Let's vacuum this up and analyze it." Coolie said.

"Captain, there is a priority phone call in your office." The yeoman said.

"This is the Captain speaking."

"Captain, this is Conroy Dillon, how is everything there?"

The Captain jumped out of his chair and nearly stood at attention.

"Just fine Mr. President. What can I do for you, sir?"

"You remember that we asked for a list of qualified officers and enlisted men to serve in the newly formed states of Mexico. I see you have submitted a Lieutenant by the name of MacKenzie. Isn't that the pilot who shot down the missile with my name on it?"

"Yes, Mr. President, he's the one."

"I thought so. Anyone with balls enough to take on an ICBM with a fighter and win the battle is good enough for me. I want him for the Liaison in Upper Mexico, but before you let him go, promote him to a field grade rank. I don't want him taking any guff from some ninety day wonder who happens to be there ahead of him."

"Yes sir, Mr. President. When should he report, Mr. President?"

"No hurry. Give him some time with his family before he starts this job. He'll need it."

"Yeoman, call Lieutenant MacKenzie to my office on the double."

Casey was on the flight deck basking in the sun when he heard his name called over the PA system. He jumped up and ran back to his room to dress for the Captain. No one ever reports to the Captain when he answers a page in anything less than full dress. "Wonder what he wants me about this time."

"Lieutenant MacKenzie reporting as ordered, Captain."

"Sit."

The Captain told Casey of the phone call he had and the gist of the conversation.

"I submitted your name and you have been picked. It will be a difficult job, but I am convinced that you can handle it. Take thirty days leave en route and have some fun with your wife and kid. Dismissed!"

On August twenty seventh 2027, Casey was promoted to Lieutenant Commander and transferred to Upper Mexico as the Military Liaison for that state. His duty station would be the new capital city of Monterrey and his boss would be the new Governor of the state.

The Secretaries of Interior and State held a conference in Mexico City with the four new Governors and their Deputies to lay out the overall plan for the rebuilding of the Mexican states.

"Upper Mexico will begin with highway and rail connections with existing US transportation routes.

One will travel down the east coast from Laredo Texas to Monterrey and then into Yucatan to the new capital city and on to the very tip. One will travel from Tucson down the west coast to Mazatlan, Guadalajara and eventually to Mexico City. The third of the main routes will travel from El Paso directly through the middle of the country to Mexico City."

"Yucatan will supply wood for ties, trestles and buildings, we will need logging operations and sawmills set up and running as soon as possible. Lower Mexico will supply minerals for road building and ballast for the rail lines and other minerals needed for construction. We will need mining operations, rock crushers and cement plants set up in this area immediately."

"Upper Mexico will make the original connections of the three highway and railroad combinations and run them south to connect to the major cities as they reach toward their ultimate destinations. Pacifica will supply labor toward the completion of this effort."

"Inside the packages you have received are maps with the proposed highways and railroads which we will be building starting immediately. Do not forget that there will be new cities and towns all along the railroads and highways all around the country. You are encouraged to populate these towns as we go with workers who will maintain and protect the new transportation routes."

"The Federal Department of Transportation will provide the funds for all of the transportation lines we have discussed here today. The states will provide all of the labor for these projects."

"Some of the first buildings to be built will be schools. As in the upper forty-eight, all children will be in schools learning to read, write and speak English and arithmetic. There will be no more Spanish spoken or taught in any of the schools."

Casey wasted no time getting ready and on his way to enjoy his leave and see his love Teresa and son Sean. The Captain said that he would be able to visit his home for a month. He entered her office at work in his Lieutenant Commander's uniform and ran into the Governor as he was ascending the stair to Teresa's office.

"Hi Casey, what are you doing here?" The Governor asked.

"Good afternoon Governor Wilhelm, I've got thirty days leave before my next assignment."

"What are you going to be doing?" He asked.

"I've been appointed the Military Liaison for the newly formed state of Upper Mexico."

"Sounds like fun, if you need any help just let me know. See you later." He said.

It wound be pointless to say Teresa was happy to see him. She was ecstatic and since it was four thirty when he entered the office and her boss thought it would be a good idea to give her the rest of the day off.

Back in Upper Mexico, the Governor was explaining the plan to all of his staff, in preparation to begin to build everything new.

"We have got to whip this state into condition, I have asked the Army Engineers to do the training of the people that we have available to us. The adults will learn to build houses and roads. There will be classes for electricians and plumbers and all the trades. They will teach farming, and most importantly, they will teach English."

"We will build schools and houses and apartments first, so all the people will have somewhere to call home. We will rebuild the State Capital Buildings since they were damaged and partially destroyed in the air attacks. We will set up Monterrey as the model for all of the other Capital cities to follow."

"We will establish public works, utilities, housing development and all other state boards. Keep in mind, this state is like the old west a hundred fifty years ago and it is our job to bring everything up to date."

Only three weeks later, the Deputy Governor stepped out in front of a speeding car in front of the interim Capital Building in Monterrey. He was DOA at the local hospital.

Casey was lying on the couch waiting for Tease to come home from work and watching a daytime soap opera when the phone rang.

"Hello?"

"Casey, this is Governor Pedro Garcia. I wouldn't call you if it were not important, but due to the death of the Deputy Governor over the weekend, I am appointing you to that position. One of the first things to do is make some traffic laws and provide police to enforce them." He said.

Casey was dumbfounded as he tried to find words on the phone.

"But."

"How soon can you be here?"

"How soon do you need me?" Casey said.

"Monday would be fine."

"It's already Thursday." Casey said.

Casey was dejected that his leave was cut short and agreed to walk with Tease the next morning to work at the Capital Building. Casey was standing at her door just ready to leave when Governor Wilhelm walked up.

"Good morning, Teresa. Good morning, Casey. You certainly have a long face. What seems to be the trouble?"

"The Deputy Governor was killed yesterday and I have been appointed to fill his position." Casey said.

"I can feel for you, that's a terrible job." He said.

Casey explained to the Governor what their mandate was and how much was to be done.

"I know a railroad construction engineer who lives here in town, he knows all about building a railroad. Let's go see him. He lives out on Hot Springs Road. Tony worked on the V&T and the UP." Governor Wilhelm said.

They drove across town to see Tony Dominguez and had a very enjoyable meeting. Tony is nearly seventy, but knows all there is to know about the railroad business. The three of them talked for two hours.

Casey took all the information Tony gave him back to Mexico with him and told his new boss, the Governor, what he had learned.

"If you think he can build the railroad for us, then get him. Take a plane and bring him back, there's an old Mirage F1C in one of the hangars on the airfield in town. Can you fly it?"

"I can fly anything that will fly." Casey said.

"Good! I thought you would say that. Gas it up and get him back here as fast as you can. I can pay him at grade six or seven I think. Take your time, but get him."

It was another opportunity to be home with Teresa for the weekend. Casey made arrangements with Tony for a Monday morning departure.

"You want me to fly in this thing?"

"It's like driving a little sports car, Tony. It'll be fun, you'll see. Don't worry, I'll be gentle on you." Casey said.

During the first meeting with Governor Garcia and Casey, Tony didn't waste any time with talk.

"We'll start in the east because it reaches Yucatan and Lower Mexico both. Wood would come by rail from the south and rails would come from the steel mill in Pueblo, Colorado from the north. That mill will supply rails, spikes, fishplates and all other steel items we will need. The first rails laid will connect Monterrey to Tampico, then on to Veracruz, then to Campeche and Merida. The final link in this section of the Texas and Yucatan Rail Road will be to Nuevo Laredo and across the border to Texas." Tony said.

Even with the best equipment, Tony has only been able to grade ten miles of new track per day because of the lack of material and trained men. They are building stations and other buildings as they go through the rough arid land. They leave people behind at each station that want to live there and new people are always ready to come to work for the railroad.

On the fifteenth of May of '28, Teresa presented Casey with a second son, William. Casey was beside himself with joy.

Carlos Casado found his way to the offices of the Schneller, Schwartz and Kidder Law Firm on McDowell Road.

"Excuse me miss, I am Carlos Casado and I have an appointment."

"Yes, Mr. Casado. Someone will be with you in just a minute."

"Good morning, I am Mitchell Cordell, let's go into this interview room and discuss your case."

"Man, the laws on sexual harassment become so stringent that you can't even wink at a woman anymore."

"From what I have here in the brief, you did more than wink. You could be looking at a life sentence if they push this through. Tell me exactly what you did and said, and what she did and said. The truth!" Mitchell said.

Carlos bared his soul to Mitchell with all the lewd details of his affair with Dulce.

"We would meet and go into the supply room where I would fondle her, and she would do nice things for me. We did that many times, it was like a mutual admiration society and we did that a couple of times a week, every week during the campaign year. She got skittish when some sour faced reporter in the media gave me a bad rap."

"The first thing we will do is to legally change your name to Charles Casado. OK, Chuck? We will do this before we start anything. Fill out and sign these forms and we will get started right away. You know of course that she has you dead to rights."

"If you get me off, I will give you anything." Carlos said.

"I will need a witness who will lie for you. Do you know someone to fit that description?"

"Yes, Dolores Trujillo was the other woman in the office that I visited regularly, and she has said more than once that she loves me."

"Perfect, get her down here to see me right away. Then we will buy off a juror, do you have enough money for that?"

"Money is very easy to find in my job."

"I see. What is it that you do?"

"I am the State Senator for District Two."

The pre trial media coverage was a gold mine for Mitchell. He dug into the bag of tricks he had learned over the years, and pulled out insinuation, innuendo and aspersion. Further along in the trial he would need belittling, deceit and vilification to serve him well, and they did.

The Trial dragged on and Mitchell milked every drop of media coverage for his benefit as well as the benefit of his client. Chuck was becoming more and more impressed with the young lawyer who had single handedly grabbed the media by their throat and stifled them.

"Charles Casado was always a model of propriety around the office and in his private life." Dolores said under oath.

"Now we must prove Dulce was paid, and that the meetings with you in the supply room were all her idea. We must make her out to be a prostitute." Mitchell said.

"I have a cop in the thirteenth precinct who owes me a favor. Will that help?"

"Perfect! That may be the straw that broke the camel's back."

"I call Sergeant Ramirez to the stand."

"Sergeant Ramirez, do you recognize the young lady sitting there at that table?"

"Yes sir, I do. That's Dulce Santana."

"Under what circumstances did you see her last?"

"She was picked up for prostitution and brought to my precinct house."

"When was this?"

"About a year ago, sir." He said.

After the trial, Chuck told all the reporters gathering around him what a great young lawyer Mitchell was, and that he couldn't have proven his innocence without him, which was the only truth told at the time. The lies were so obvious it's a wonder the jurors didn't notice, but then people hear what they want to hear and no more.

Driving away from the courthouse in the limousine after the trial Carlos Casado asked Mitchell the one question Mitchell was waiting for all these years.

"How can I pay you?"

"I want to be Mayor of Phoenix." Mitchell said.

"I can do that."

The trial ended late in '28 and it was only a few months before Mitchell and Chuck Casado began their collaborative campaign to elect Mitchell as mayor in earnest.

During the winter, early in '29, Canada's economic system collapsed, much like the crash of '15 in the US.

There had been an unusually long severe winter in the plains of Canada. Crops didn't get put in as they should, there may not be a harvest of the crops that were planted and a loss of confidence by the people and big companies all around the country in the government and the stock market caused everything to fall at the same time. The President of Canada put in an urgent call to Conroy Dillon for help.

"We need about five billion dollars to get this problem cleared. That is an early estimate, it could be much more."

President Dillon ordered his staff to drop everything and immediately get to work on the Canada problem. As it turned out, the United States couldn't bail out Canada. It took far too much money, but Conroy came up with a alternate answer.

"My advisers have come up with another solution, but it could be a bit distasteful to many of your people. We could annex Canada into the United States, then we would really be the United States of America."

"I'll get back to you."

Canadian President Francois Ulrich and his Cabinet and staff spent four days and nights together in the Capital agonizing over the possible effects of such a move as this, but finally when the vote was taken, the decision was made. Each province will become a state and another star added to the US flag. The states were entered beginning in the east to the west right across the country.

A team of five men was sent from the US government to each state to handle the transition. There were the new Governor and Lieutenant Governor, the Attorney General, Speaker of the House and the Press Secretary.

"Good evening. This is World News Tonight for May thirteenth, 2029. The President of Canada, Francois Ulrich, met with US President Conroy Dillon to work out details and announce a peaceful annexation of Canada and all the islands off shore into the United States of America."

"May I help you sir?" Casey asked the thin young man dressed in a black double breasted pinstripe suit.

"Hi, I'm Henry Jones from the State Department and it is my job to translate every unpronounceable Spanish name to the English meaning if possible. I was told you would be able to help me."

Casey grew up with Spanish as his second language and he knows how funny this kind of thing can be. Casey couldn't help himself, he tried but the laughter just took over.

"Do you think this is funny? Translate this! Coatzacoalcos, Tlaxcalan, Tlatelolca, Xochimilco."

Pronouncing those names is funny even when you know how to speak the language, but this wimp from Washington with his eastern twang trying to pronounce possibly the hardest names in the world was so funny Casey couldn't contain himself.

"Listen kid, come over here and sit down." Casey was still laughing.

Casey gave Henry Jones a short lesson in Spanish and told him not to try to translate the names.

"Just make up your own names. No one will know but you. And no one will care either."

The annexation of Greenland was an obvious choice to President Dillon's Cabinet.

"We've already added Canada and Greenland is a province of Denmark, they can't be very interested in it."

Greenland is more than three times the size of Texas and is only ten miles from Canada at one point. It is one large snow covered island of 840,000 square miles in area. Not the most inviting place in the world with a high temperature of fifty degrees in the south during July.

Denmark, of course, decided not to have a war with the United States over the frozen island and the annexation continued very peacefully. The name of the capital city, Godthab, was changed to Greenland City. Eventually all cities in the new state will be renamed with English names.

Chapter 8

The Earthquake

January 2030

Monterrey was a perfect selection for the Capital City of Upper Mexico. It was Mexico's third largest city with many industries already operating there. Spanish songs of love and romance can be heard in concerts and parades on a regular basis.

The tall buildings share space along the streets with quaint little shops offering finely crafted jewelry of silver and turquoise, hand painted pottery and many other items that the maker has put his talent into. Tours of the bull ring, glass factories, the brewery and the Bishop's Palace are easily arranged.

But far and away, the place Casey most liked was the visit to Huasteca Canyon. The rough drive on the unimproved dirt road was nothing compared to the geological heaven of unusual and colorful formations that was waiting for him when he arrived.

It was a cool January day in Monterrey when the Governor and Casey were exploring options for making the new state better.

"Listen Casey, my name is Pedro Ignacio Garcia. Since we're going to be working together, why don't you call me Pete, all my friends do. And no funny stuff with the initials, either. Let me tell you a story."

"There used to be a railroad which ran from a little town across the river from Presidio, Texas named Ojinaga, Upper Mexico. The stories about this railroad have said that it passed through seventy-three tunnels and crossed four miles of bridges while crossing Upper Mexico to the Pacific. In the mountains, the tracks were said to run along a deep copper canyon where, according to the legend, gold was said to be found by prospectors years ago."

"In the past, the President of Mexico had heard these stories and sent soldiers and civilians out to find the tracks of the abandoned roadbed or the gold, but nothing was ever found."

Casey celebrated his thirtieth birthday at the Capital building the same day that Tony and his track gang arrived in Veracruz from the north. It would only be a few more weeks until the railroad reached Evergreen and the lumber mills.

Later in the week, the Governor summoned Tony to his office to tell him about the trip through the state. Tony came up from Veracruz in his private railcar for the meeting and Governor Garcia explained.

"I would like for you and Tony make an inspection tour of the state to find the best route for both rail and highway construction. And disregard any fairy tales about railroads and gold mines you might hear on the way. I'd also like to have your ideas for what we should be making the priorities for the state."

"I don't want to fly in that thing he calls a sports car with him again. No thank you, sir. Not me!" Tony said.

Tony finally relented when Pete decided that the trip would be made in a helicopter that was also available at the airport. Tony held on for dear life for the first hour or so, then he decided that Casey wasn't going to throw him out onto the ground. They flew from Monterrey to Torreon viewing the route carefully. Then north to Chihuahua, which was renamed Littleton, a much longer and more interesting leg of the journey.

The trip turned out to be a lot of fun for Tony and Casey, they spent the first day studying the terrain of Upper Mexico and planning for future construction.

Mitchell Cordel and Chuck Casado spent many hours and dollars on the campaign last year and the alliance between them did eventually bear fruit. It was true that money and muscle was the major reason that, on January twentieth, Mitchell was sworn in as the Mayor of Phoenix.

"The campaign lasted nearly all year, but it was worth it. I'm Mayor of Phoenix now. Now it begins for us, Chuck. Now it begins!" Mitchell said.

It was around noon of the second day of Casey and Tony's inspection trip when the dispatcher called Casey on the phone.

"Commander, I have a priority call for you from NASA, I'll put it through."

"Commander MacKenzie speaking."

"Hey Casey, its Chuck Kinkaid. How's it going?"

"Chuck, you caught me at two thousand feet over Guaymas. I'm on my way up the coast toward Yuma. What can I do for you?"

"You knew that I worked for NASA didn't you?"

"No I didn't. Why do you mention it?"

"Bruce Gardner and I have been working very closely with a noted scientist on his latest invention, and - - - ."

Casey interrupted him.

"Don't forget, the phone you're talking on is not secure, so be careful what you say."

"Sorry, I forgot, let me make this short then. Would you be interested in being the pilot for the space station shuttle and help us test this new invention?" He asked.

"I might, but do you think I can fly good enough for them. I'm not too special."

"Your modesty is showing. Remember, I have seen your - - ."

"Chuck! Stop! There has been an earthquake under the Gulf of California! It is occurring right now!"

"Dispatcher! Get on the emergency land line to Yuma. Tell them there is a huge wave running up the gulf toward them and they have only a couple of hours or so to evacuate the city. Be sure to tell them to evacuate to the east. There's higher ground there. Hurry!"

Casey was yelling into the microphone as he watched the water rise in the Gulf and overtake everything in its path. The water moved north at an incredible pace, washing the shore clean of all life.

"I'll stay on station and on the phone as long as our fuel holds out. This must have been a big one, the wave is big and getting bigger and its building as it goes. Strap yourself in Tony, it might get a little bumpy."

About five minutes later, they heard the radio announcer say, "We interrupt this program with a bulletin from the National Seismographic Laboratory in Boulder, Colorado. There has been an enormous earthquake centered off shore near Guaymas, Upper Mexico. The quake was so large that it recorded off the Richter scale."

Casey tried to fly ahead of the wave in order to notify other towns along the way with his loud speakers mounted under the aircraft. Speaking in Spanish, he told everyone he saw to run for the hills. The wave swept along the gulf at nearly two hundred miles per hour and destroyed everything on the beach on both sides as it moved north.

About twenty or thirty thousand residents of Yuma believed the television and radio announcements and evacuated immediately. Another twenty or thirty thousand were moving out of town when the wave entered the south part of town. There was no chance of saving anyone in the immediate path of the oncoming water. Now there is a mile wide deep channel from the gulf into the Mojave Desert.

No one really believes the Federal Government actually makes a concerted effort to be stupid. The problem is that the bureaucrats are always right and never seem to be able to see the other side of anything. Maybe that's just the way it works out, but for over a decade now the public has been flying and dying in the Commutercopter. Fred had a fantastic idea when he designed the CC, but none of the necessary controls or safeguards were put in place by the government, and the design was downgraded by the automakers in order to provide more profit.

Because of the Commutercopter, trucks, bicycles and motorcycles were the only vehicles left on the streets and roads. The presence of automobiles had dwindled to nothing, but the death rate rose to over fifty thousand every year. Casey made sure to tell Teresa not to get a CC and keep that old pickup. Teresa bought a brand new pickup for herself a few years ago, and she wasn't going to give it up.

All repair parts for all automobiles have been discontinued and auto parts stores have closed. Now, when an automobile is wrecked or it just stops running, it goes out of commission, it would be taken to the junkyard where the metal parts were melted down and could be later recycled into weapons or Commutercopter parts.

It was February twenty first of 2030 that a giant earthquake, so large it was off the Richter scale, began under the gulf of California and traveled north under the gulf and along the Colorado river into the American Desert. The quake pushed a wall of water before it that rose to nearly fifty feet.

This immense tidal wave rushed into the lower Colorado River valley where the river enters the gulf with such force that everything in its path was completely destroyed and the land was devastated. The water continued to push north across the hot sand in all directions.

This first gigantic tremor was predicted many years ago by geologists and seismologists who had been studying the tremors and shaking of the earth. However what followed was a surprise to everyone in the earth-watching community.

The main tremor was immediately followed by a secondary tremor that registered over seven, centered in a little town of Lagunitas, on the California and Arizona border along the Colorado River. It ripped a huge gash in the earth along the Colorado River which allowed the water from the Gulf of California to begin to flow into the desert.

A tertiary tremor nearly as large as the first two finished the series of events with a fury when the sands of the Mojave Desert dropped to a level more than fifty feet below sea level.

Word spread quickly to the news media that Casey was an observer to the catastrophic event and there was a media circus at the airport when he and Tony returned to Monterrey from their trip.

When asked by one of the reporters about the event, Casey said, "The water appeared to rise in the Gulf of California and flow north. Just as the crest of the wave was about to reach the end of the gulf, the earth split and a trough appeared at the northern end of the gulf.

As the water was rushing into the trough formed by the earthquake, I could see the land to the north appear to begin to sink in front of the advancing water. The water rushed in with a tremendous force and washed everything from its path and totally and completely flooded the immediate area."

"Commander, did you hear the radio broadcast of the warning about the event?"

"Yes, I remember the broadcast about the earthquake. The bulletin came on the radio about five minutes after we saw it happen. Most of their information was correct from what I could see from my vantage point. It happened right in front of us."

The President declared the whole area a disaster area. The Red Cross brought food and helped people to shelters, and there were boats on the newly formed lake trying to rescue what people there might be in the water, but there were none. The only people that got out with there lives were the ones who started running as soon as they saw the water.

A short summation of the toll that the quake took covers many areas. Interstate Forty as well as many other roads run straight into the water. The bridges across the Colorado River stop at the edge of the lake.

Rail and road service is cut in all directions, towns like Blythe, Brawley, El Centro and Mexicali, California were completely destroyed or covered. The Salton Sea, originally two hundred thirty five feet below sea level, was filled again. The Imperial Valley was also filled with the result that all the crops were lost, and thousands of people were lost.

Once things finally got started with the railroad later in the spring, they hummed right along, equipment began to roll in on trucks from the Upper Forty Eight. The rock crusher was one of the first items to be transported into the area.

It was located, erected and set up in the rock quarry located near a town named Orizaba. It began production in February. Ballast and other mineral products started to roll out in large quantities, and the town was renamed Rockville.

The lumber mill took much longer to locate, build and begin operation. Lumberjacks had to be trained, skids had to be built and many smaller tasks of the logging business had to be performed before the lumber mill could begin production.

The sawmill and tie producing operation was built near a town named Minatitlan, in Yucatan. Production did finally become a reality last year and ties are being produced and shipped. The town was later re-named Evergreen for the surrounding forests.

Trucks loaded with ballast arrived first from Rockville, then trucks loaded with ties arrived from Evergreen, trucks loaded with rails, spikes and fishplates arrived from Pueblo and the railroad was moving. Tony and his track gangs pushed day in and day out from Monterrey south toward their goal.

Roger Pond called Casey late in May to ask if he would come to NASA and discuss joining the space program. Casey had given it some thought since Chuck had talked to him that day and Casey told him that he would be happy to visit Houston. Chuck and Bruce met Casey at the airport to escort him to the lab and Roger's office.

"Come with us and meet Dr. Kuhlmann, you have got to see this invention and meet him, it'll just freak you out!" Chuck always gets excited when he talks about Spector.

Chuck and Bruce set up a test of Spector for Casey, but Casey had no idea he would be the one to test it. Coolie got the equipment ready as the other two prepared Casey for the test.

When everyone was ready, Coolie began the countdown.

FLASH!

Casey was gone for two hours. When he came back he had a look of disbelief on his face. Collie and the others were very insistent that he explain everything he saw and did while he was wherever he was.

"Well, what do you think?" Chuck asked.

"You know, if you guys can get this thing perfected so I could go back and do a few things, I'd be interested in helping any way I could." Casey said.

Mitchell had consented to a meeting with Delmer Scott at his office in June. Mitchell didn't like Delmer much, he reminded him of a little rat, but he worked for NASA and was just devious enough to agree to almost anything Mitchell wanted, for a price.

"This is the best weapon there ever was, Sir." Delmer told Mitchell what he had seen in Roger Pond's office. "He aimed it at him and Flash he was gone. Just disappeared."

"How does this affect me?" Mitchell asked.

"I can get it easy, but it's pretty big."

"How big?"

"It will take two suitcases and a briefcase to carry it all."

"We can't use it when it's that big. Get someone to make it smaller. Make it fit into a small container so we can use it."

"Mr. Cordel, Sir. I know a company that can reverse engineer and manufacture this device for us. The company is California Optical Technical Electronics Company, (COPTEK). But it'll be expensive."

"How much?"

"I'll find out." Delmer said.

It wasn't hard for Delmer and two cohorts to slip into the building and steal the Spector that Sunday afternoon. Delmer had keys for most of the doors and there were four wheel carts to move the heavy items sitting all around the labs. Just as the shift was ending, they casually walked out with it looking like they should have been carrying the suitcases.

Monday morning the NASA Security Office called Roger Pond to ask if anyone had been authorized into the lab on the sixth floor.

"Why do you ask?"

"The items that were set up on the testing tables there Friday are not there now, sir." The guard said.

"Damn!"

Later that Monday, Coolie, Bruce, Chuck and Ken were summoned to Roger's office and notified that they would have to build another and NASA will help.

"How could such a theft as this have happened here?"

"Security is working on it, but I can't come right out and tell them what was taken. They'd put me away. This will be a tough one."

"What do you want us to do?" Coolie asked.

"You may work here or in your private lab in your home if you wish." Roger said.

"Let's all go to Redlake, it'll be quiet." Bruce said.

"It should be. It's the end of the world." Chuck said.

Tony and his railroad engineers are back to laying tracks for the railroad down the east coast, completing the leg from Monterrey to Laredo.

Many small buildings must be built along the right-of-way, both freight and passenger stations and the multitude of repair and maintenance buildings necessary to keep a railroad moving.

At the same time, a crew was finishing the rebuilding of the Capital buildings and the airport facilities in Monterrey. Even with all the laborers working day and night, it will be many more weeks before it is finished.

In order to celebrate the Fourth of July properly, Casey flew up to Carson City and brought Teresa and the kids down to Monterrey for a visit. They all stayed in the apartment in the capital just like a real family for a whole week during summer vacation.

"I really like having you around all the time, we should do this more often." Teresa said.

"I agree completely. Now come here and give me a hug."

Her job is going better all the time, she is making a little headway on a new strain of corn and wheat that will grow on the Nevada desert and flourish on the little precipitation. Now that there is the lake close by, consequently Nevada gets more rain and her corn and wheat are covering the Nevada farmlands across the state like a blanket.

It was the first year that El Nino had been active since its tumultuous episode in '98 and storms had been pounding the shores from Peru to Oregon. The first six named storms became Category One and Two on the Saffir-Simpson Scale and blew themselves out in the Pacific Ocean with high winds affecting shipping lanes and producing high waves at the shorelines.

Gloria was different. Tropical depression Gloria developed into Hurricane Gloria off shore west of Peru and moved around in circles as if it would also blow itself out, but on Halloween, Gloria drew a bead on Pacifica and came roaring across the little peninsula. Crossing the land mass drew Gloria down from a Category Four to a Category Three storm, but that didn't stop her. The warm waters of the Gulf strengthened the storm again and it moved north into the lower part of California.

Meteorologists and weather forecasters around the country tried to predict what this storm would do and when it would do it, but to no avail. It seemed that Gloria had a mind of her own.

Since November is a colder part of the year and cold fronts normally push south from Canada into the Continental US, it wasn't surprising to see this happening. As Gloria was driving north, a cold front was dropping down from Canada and the two met over the ghost town of Needles, California.

Gloria stalled against the strong, wide cold front and the rain continued to fall heavily. The rain fell from Gloria into the new depression in the desert in sheets.

After several days of hard rain, Gloria finally dropped almost all the water she was carrying and collapsed into a series of small clouds. What was left was carried along with the cold front and dissipated across the Midwest.

The storm had dropped millions of gallons of water into the desert and filled it all the way to Death Valley. Areas like China Lake, Twenty Nine Palms and Devil's Playground are only a faint memory now, those areas were lost under the new lake forever. All the lowest points became filled with water and soon the desert was completely covered. Lake Mojave was complete.

Tony and his crews had worked tirelessly and have completed the Mexico East Coast RR and they have started working on the connection from Monterrey to Torreon to the Central Mexico RR. The terrain is generally level and work proceeded at a steady pace, but as always, all the extra off-line building continued to take more time.

A great exodus of all the Indian peoples living in the southwest started immediately and continued for many months as they marched northward. From time to time, small groups would break off from the main contingent and settle in certain areas of the country, but for the most part, the migration continued north well into Canada.

During the migration, Teresa's family is moving out of the desert lands along with thousands of others. They were spread across the desert, now all of them are moving to the north in a single group. They all gathered together for one night at Teresa's house in Carson City when Casey was home for a weekend off.

"Where will you go?" Teresa asked.

"North is the only direction we have left, my dear." Judge said.

"Listen Grandfather, I know a place. Go north until you find my name on the river and the mountains. Look at this map." Casey said.

Casey pointed to the area he was describing to Judge.

"My father told me of this special place when I was very young. He said it was a special, almost magical place. Stop there and settle down for a time. This is where you can build your town. You will be safe there. Tease and I will come to visit soon."

Chapter 9

The Greek Letter, Theta

January 2031

Governor Pete has given Casey free rein to come and go to Carson City as often as he wished. Now that Teresa's family have all moved to Canada, she has been devoting more of her thoughts and actions toward growing food and the two boys.

Since Lake Mojave filled up, the jet stream has been carrying more moisture into Nevada and the new strains of seeds that Teresa has developed are growing better than ever. The southwest border of the state has turned green and there have even been fruit trees planted in orchards near Las Vegas.

Casey enjoys flying that Mirage back and forth on a regular basis to see the love of his life and his two wonderful boys. He has that old Dodge pickup parked in the lot at the airport waiting for him when he lands.

Usually he has some stories of the new railroads and now that the MEC is finished, construction of the interstate highway has begun in a strip next to the railroad. But today he has something special to tell Tease.

"I went to Houston to NASA. They asked me if I wanted to fly the space shuttle. Boy would I like to do that!"

"It sounds like you have already accepted the job."
She said.

"No. I wanted to tell you about it before I took it."

"That's what I said."

Tease loved to pick on Casey, but most of all she loved to love him. She was really enjoying these once a week visits, and thought she could get used to having him around all the time, but then he was packing to go again. Maybe soon.

It's a good thing Dr. Kuhlmann left all the drawings and notes for the Spector design back at his home in Redlake. Bruce, Chuck and Ken are pouring over every tiny bit of each drawing in preparation to building a new prototype.

Coolie has been studying the schematics trying to find that one thing that would allow them to go to the past and return. The prototype would send something, or someone, to the past, but there was no way to get it back, and without the memory module, the person wouldn't know why they were in the past. Maybe they wouldn't even know where they were.

"Look! This part was drawn in backwards on the schematic. I wonder if it was in backwards on the prototype. It would be interesting to see what it would do. I'll have to work on that." Coolie said.

Coolie gets pretty enthusiastic when he finds an answer and begins to talk to himself when he does. Coolie was filled with joy that he had found a mistake in the schematic drawing, but was it also wrong in the original model? Coolie stumbled onto something during the intense study of the drawings, formulas and schematics.

"I think I can adjust the time by changing this voltage a little, maybe we can put a variable resistor here, or maybe here." Collie is pointing at each part on the drawing with his red pencil and talking to any one who would listen.

He knew that he must build a new device, and that they must figure out the problem that stands in the way of completion.

"I've got it!" He said.

That woke them up. They came to see what he was talking about.

"We have to change this." He said.

He was pointing with his red pencil at the drawing. They didn't know what it was that they had to change, but Coolie did, and he went on his way finishing the task at hand. Coolie worked through the night and sometime in the early afternoon he made an exclamation.

"Now it will work!" He said.

The first device he made couldn't go to the past when they had tried that experiment with the girl. Bruce, Chuck and Ken had a new feeling to consummate the task at hand, now that Coolie seemed to find the mistake in the design. The four of them worked tirelessly for two months redesigning and rebuilding the new Spector.

When it was completed and sitting on the table in the middle of the dining room, Chuck made an interesting observation.

"If this thing is going to propel a spacecraft through time, shouldn't we be assembling it onto a craft and outfitting the pilot with the memory module into his headset?" Chuck doesn't often come up with the idea of the week, but this time he did.

"We need an aircraft engineer who will help us with this." Ken said.

"I know just the one." Chuck said.

"Not Casey." Bruce asked.

"No. Fred Goss, the guy that invented the Commutercopter." Chuck said. "I met him at his Colorado home several years ago."

"Don't forget! We will need to do more tests on this design with someone before we take it into space." Coolie said.

"I know just the one to help us test it. Remember the girl, she was willing to do a lot more than what we wanted last time. Besides, I think she noticed how charming and good looking I am and would like to do some special tests with me." Chuck said.

The other three made obscene sounds and razzed him, but he was right. Yvonne did the first test and was willing to go a lot farther than she did, but they didn't ask.

"Chuck of the Yukon will volunteer his valuable time to go to town and rescue the fair maid from the life of drudgery of her present existence and introduce her to the man of her dreams, which is of course, 'Chuck of the Yukon'."

Chuck made his voice sound like an old-time radio announcer for an adventure show, and with that he exited stage right just like a vaudeville player to the front door of the house with his parka out into the snow.

"He needs a rest." Bruce said.

"Or a woman." Ken said.

"Maybe both." Coolie said.

They all laughed.

Now that cement, sand and aggregate are being delivered by the MEC RR to the exact site where the construction of the interstate highway has begun, the highway construction is going much faster.

The connection from Laredo, Texas to Monterrey is complete and Tony's new railroad, the Central of Mexico, is pushing south from Torreon. Construction of the Interstate highway will follow the tracks all the way to the Caribbean.

Governor Pete called Tony for an update and some words of encouragement for Tony.

"Tony, you're making great strides toward the completion of our new transportation system. Keep up the good work."

Delmer entered the Offices of COPTEK with a big smile on his face and two big suitcases in his hands.

"May I help you, sir?" The receptionist said.

"I came to see Daniel O'Malley."

"Do you have an appointment, sir?"

"No. He's my brother-in-law and I have a big contract for him."

The receptionist showed Delmer a seat and called her boss immediately. Dan hurried to the reception area.

"Delmer! How good to see you. What's this Judith tells me about a big contract?"

"Let's go sit down somewhere private where we can talk."

"Sure. Where are my manners? Judith, would you have someone bring something to drink and some snacks to my office for Delmer and I."

Daniel O'Malley organized California Optical Technical Electronics Company, COPTEK, from nothing but an idea and an abandoned gas station. Now he builds everything there is in optics and electronics in a much larger facility, and makes a lot of money doing it. Delmer had the two suitcases and the briefcase with him and opened them on the table in Dan's office.

"This is the item." Delmer put the various items of the stolen Spector on the table for Dan to examine. "The buyer wants you to make this much smaller, it should fit into something about the size of this."

Delmer produced an old four by five format camera from the suitcase, like a photographer would use when he was doing exteriors.

"The buyer wants a hard price from you before you start. When can you have it?"

"Give me two or three weeks." Dan said.

Dan knew his business and he knew a lot about other peoples business too. This device that Delmer had dropped in his lap didn't look right, maybe he would factor in some contingency costs just to cover the ifs that might pop up out of nowhere. Dan filled out all the paperwork for the contract and listed Delmer under "Salesman".

"This should be a big commission for you." Dan said.

"Yes and it should continue for a lot more units." Delmer said.

He called in his engineers and explained the job to them and told them to give him a price to reverse engineer the device and another price to build it.

"And don't waste any time." Daniel said.

Casey is coming home every weekend and Teresa is glad to have him around for two whole days and three nights.

"I could get used to this, honey."

"I could too, Tease. I just love being with you on these weekends. Hang on, we've both got a lot of work to do, it won't be long, I think."

The first four Spectors that Delmer picked up from **COPTEK** were fitted into the Hasselblad four by five inch format cameras with bellows and tripod. The whole thing measures about ten by six by seven inches high.

The power supply that is needed to operate the Spector unit was quite large and was fitted into a leather covered metal box made to look like a film case with the word "Film" labeled on it.

Mitchell wasn't very happy about the price of $26,450 each, and he didn't much like trusting that ratty little Delmer with this kind of project, but he had no other source for the devices.

Delmer personally delivered all four of the completed Spectors to the Office of the Mayor of

Phoenix. Delmer is an entrepreneur, he works at NASA in the mail room and he knows everything that goes on there.

But he sells information and takes every opportunity to make a buck. Naturally Delmer wasn't carrying the trunk with the cameras, his two "assistants" were doing the heavy labor.

Mitchell ushered them into his office and as soon as the trunk was placed in the center of the floor, Delmer dismissed his men for the day.

Mitchell wanted to test it right then, but Delmer would have to show him how to set it up. Several minutes later, Mitchell called his secretary on the intercom.

"Miss Greene, get that guy that was complaining about city policy over here right away."

While they waited, Delmer explained what he knew of the new weapon. Thirty-five minutes later Miss Greene announced that James Jackson had entered the office.

"Send him right in."

"Stand over here, James, I want to get your picture."

FLASH!

Once their eyes came back to normal, Mitchell and Delmer saw that the only thing left in that room of James Jackson was his shadow on the floor and wall.

"There now, that fixes that complaint. Wow! Does that ever work nice! There's your check." Mitchell said pointing toward the desk.

Delmer left his card for future orders on the desk and picked up the check that was laying there. Delmer conveniently forgot to mention that he gets ten percent of the sale for his commission, and the commission from a hundred and five thousand eight hundred dollars would come in handy right now.

Casey is flying the Mirage weekly on a straight route between Monterrey and Carson City. As a sort of self-entertainment during the flights, sometimes Casey will do lots of fancy flying over the barren areas of Upper Mexico and Arizona.

As always, Teresa is glad to have him home more often, and greets him with hugs and kisses. She always tells him that she could get used to this. The truth is he could too.

"Miss Greene, you may make those calls for me now."

"Hello?"

"Hello Bobby, this is Mitchell Cordel, Mayor of Phoenix. I have belonged to our local group here in Phoenix since seventh grade. I wonder if you could visit me here at my office. I have something very special and new for you to see."

"Can you tell me what this new thing is?" Bobby asked.

"No sir, I can't. You know how words seem to leak out."

"Yes, I see. How about Friday May second?"

"Good, I'll clear the whole day and we will have lunch after a small demonstration."

"Your second call is waiting on line three, Mr. Mayor."

"This is Mitchell Cordel. How are you Jeremy?"

"Doing well Mitchell. How can I help you?" Jeremy asked.

"I would like for you to come visit me here at my office. I've cleared the whole day of May second for this."

"What's it all about?"

"Trust me. I have something to show you and much to talk about."

"All right, I'll be there."

"Casey my darling, you make my life complete. I knew that we were soul mates way back in grade school. You always seem to know what I'm thinking, sometimes even before I'm thinking it."

"Yes and I know what you're thinking right now too, and I'm shocked that you'd want to do that in the middle of the day, too." Casey laughed and held up his hands in mock alarm as Tease's face became red.

"That's not what I was thinking either, and you know it."

"You should have been."

Friday May second would be a very special day for Mitchell. Robert Nash and Jeremy Rodgers are coming a long way for a private meeting and are expecting to see something very special.

"Mr. Mayor, the two men are here for the meeting." His secretary said over the intercom.

"No calls or appointments from anyone all day. No one! Send them in."

Both men were dressed in fine suits and ties and looked like very important people.

"Good morning gentlemen. Won't you have a seat? Let me make the introductions. This is Robert Nash, the Imperial Wizard."

"You can call me Bobby, all my friends do."

"This is Jeremy Rodgers, the General of the American Militia."

"My friends call me Jolly. Well Mitchell, what do you have for us today?"

They shook hands and took the drinks that Mitchell had prepared.

Mitchell had one of the cameras with the "film pack" connected already set up on a tripod in the same place where he had used it on James Jackson earlier. He explained in as much detail as he could, everything he knew about the camera.

"Let's see what it can do."

"Put these dark glasses on, you'll need them."

"Miss Greene, is Pedro Hernandez there waiting?"

"Yes sir, he is."

"Good, send him in, hang up the 'Do Not Disturb' sign and go on to lunch."

The door opened and Pedro entered the room.

"Pedro, would you please stand here? I want to take your picture."

Pedro stood where the Mayor indicated.

"Now watch this." He said to the two men sitting at the back of the room.

FLASH!

Pedro disappeared just like James had disappeared earlier.

"Wow!"

"I have four of these, and plan to buy many more. Each camera must be recharged for an hour before firing, but I calculate we can take four or five pictures a day, seven days a week with each camera.

I will dispatch eight men to the surrounding states to give it the final test. They will report back to me on every little detail of the operation of these devices. Of course, they will start with those people in influential jobs. Once they are eliminated, our people will fill them."

"What do you call this thing."

"It's just 'Our Camera', nothing more."

"Where did you get the money?"

"Oh that. I took it out of the City Employees Retirement Fund. They won't be needing it." Mitchell said.

"Nice going!"

"You boys are going to ante up, aren't you?"

"You bet! How much?"

"They are thirty grand each, you can pick them up here in four weeks. How many do you want?"

During the next several months, Mitchell skimmed money from the Federal Highways Fund to buy four more cameras, and State Senator Carlos "Chuck" Casado held a big political dinner at a hundred dollars a plate and collected enough to buy four more.

Arizona, Nevada, Upper Mexico and Southern California are beginning to sprout green in various places around the new lake because of the tremendous influx of water. The weather patterns have brought moisture off the lake and into Southern Nevada and Utah and green is the newest color there as well.

Casey and Tony were working every day trying to get the new transportation system to the point where it didn't occupy their every thought and action. Casey wanted to have the time to think about and visit Tease a lot more often.

It wouldn't have been hard for Chuck to find Yvonne. She works in the box office at the only movie theater in town. She is five feet eight with long curly blonde hair and blue eyes and a very beautiful face and figure. It's not like she would go unnoticed when she was not holed up in that little place selling tickets. Chuck knew who he was looking for and it didn't take him long to find her.

"Hi. I haven't seen you in a long time. You're not going to do something silly like last time are you?"

"No. Actually I came to ask if you would like to have dinner with me." Chuck said.

"I'd love to, but I have one more show to sell before I can go. Can you wait?"

"Can I? You bet! I mean, of course I can wait for you. Where should I wait?"

"Why don't I meet you there across the street in the 'Sunshine' bar? There, see?" Yvonne pointed and Chuck followed her direction.

Chuck waited dutifully in the bar and in about an hour she bounced through the door and walked over to the table and leaned over and kissed him. When she sat on the chair next to him a Sousa Band could have been playing, Chuck wouldn't have noticed. Chuck was sure he ate something, but not quite sure what it was.

Yvonne talked and Chuck smiled while they ate and danced, until she said, "I'm kind of tired, will you take me home now?"

"Where the hell have you been? Bruce asked.

"I told you I was going out to find her." Chuck said.

Chuck said it with a smile. Chuck has had a smile on his face ever since that first kiss Yvonne gave him.

"That was last week. What took you - so - long? Oh never mind."

"I found her didn't I?"

Chuck and Yvonne sat on the couch and held hands and smiled while the others finished what they were doing. Bruce and Chuck are only days apart in their birthdays, but Bruce acts like a father to Chuck sometimes.

Coolie gave Chuck and Yvonne extremely specific instructions prior to their excursion into the past. Chuck and Yvonne will go back together a year and stay for four hours and return.

"We have built two memory modules for you. Walk around, write something, eat, drink, exercise, drive a car, do everything you can for the experience of it, try everything. I need to know if there is anything you can't do."

"OK, let's go. Is everyone ready?"

Chuck and Yvonne stood where they were told, with their arms around each other.

FLASH!

Chuck and Yvonne were gone for four hours into the past of one year before. They were happy to follow Coolie's orders to the letter. They had dinner and a drink together in one of the best restaurants in town.

They talked to people as they walked along the street to where she had parked her car and they drove her car to her house where they had another mutually agreeable experience. Later they sat on her couch and relaxed with each other.

Suddenly they returned to the dining room of Coolie's house. Coolie and the others began to ask all the questions they needed answered. Chuck and Yvonne sat on the couch together and told them in great detail everything they had done for the past four hours.

"It was a real blessing, having these memory modules. It took us a few minutes to listen to the recording, but once it was finished, we knew what we had to do."

"Now one last thing, Chuck. We need Fred Goss's address and phone. You forgot to give that to us earlier." Ken said.

Chuck wrote the address on the pad on the coffee table as Ken brought in the day's newspaper and put it on the coffee table next to the pad.

"Look at that headline on today's paper." Bruce said.

Ken handed the newspaper to them. The headline read, "Strange Shadows Seen in Downtown Dallas."

"Do you know what this means. Someone out there has Spector and is using it as a weapon. We've got to go to Dallas."

The article went on to tell about the strange disappearances of people in Dallas and other places around the country. There were several photos of the strange 'shadows' on the ground, buildings and on other solid objects.

"Come on, I'll take you home." Chuck said to Yvonne. "We're going to Dallas, then back to NASA."

On the drive across town Chuck asked Yvonne to come back to Houston with him.

"I need you. You make me feel special." He said.

"No, I can't. My folks are here. Don't worry, I'll be here when you want me. You know how to find me. Maybe you might like it here if there was someone that loved you here with you." Yvonne said.

"Tony has the Central of Mexico Railroad up to El Paso, the highway is ready to make a connection with the Interstate in Texas." Casey told her.

"Have I told you how much I love you and how much I love having you home on the weekends?" She said.

"I never get tired of hearing that, Tease." He said.

Bruce, Chuck, Ken and Coolie knew immediately what made the shadows on the ground and went to

Dallas to investigate. Someone is using the Spector they stole from NASA.

"There were people standing in these shadows before they disappeared."

"It looks like we have a maniac on the loose."

Bags of material were swept from the shadows on the ground and buildings. These will be analyzed for everything we know of by Coolie and his crew.

"These particles were on the people who were standing in the shadows when the Spector fired.

By using his radiacmeter, Coolie found a very strange radioactive signature in the shadows. One he had not seen before. Many tests were run and the scientists discovered that they had a new radioactive particle that none of them had ever seen before on their hands.

As soon as Coolie returned to the NASA lab, he began to call all the members of the scientific community who he knew or had any dealings with in the past. Three hours later, he finally found someone who knew the answer, Dr. John Lucas.

"They came from where? John? Are you sure?"

"Back in 2003, many tests were run and the scientists working on these projects discovered that they had a new radioactive particle that none of them had ever seen before on their hands. It was dubbed with the Greek letter "Theta" by Dr. William Ashford. Theta has long stood for the unknown in formulas and scientific jargon." Dr. Lucas said.

"Then all this is due to a microscopic particle brought here from a passing celestial body and transmitted around the world - how?"

"The only vehicle I can understand that could achieve this feat, Hermann, is the natural flowing jetstream."

Back at NASA, the four of them took all the debris they swept up from the shadows in Dallas and began to run every test known. Coolie modified a radiacmeter to detect the theta particle, he called it a Thetiacmeter.

Thanksgiving was always a happy time for Casey and Teresa. She would cook a big dinner and both of them would eat too much and later curl up together on the couch amid a lot of hugging and kissing and laughter.

This Thanksgiving was no different, except Tease had said that the hugging and "other stuff" would have to wait till the kids went to bed. Tease was always as good as her word, once the kids went to bed, she curled up on his lap and whispered into his ear. "Hi there. Do I know you?"

Mitchell assembled his four two man teams and explained how to operate the cameras and gave them a few last words of advice before they left.

"Listen! Don't let anyone see you doing this. Do it around noon on a bright day so the flash isn't so noticeable and remember only Indians, Mexicans, blacks and black haired Europeans are to be purified."

It was almost Christmas when Casey flew into the Carson City Airport. He parked his plane in the usual spot and walked to his waiting Dodge pickup, which also was parked in the usual place. It was a leisurely drive in the bright sunny December day. He parked in the drive at the front of the house and walked up onto the porch.

What a strange look there was about the porch, Casey thought, there was what looked like a shadow on the floor and wall of the porch. The door was open and the radio was playing.

"I wonder where Tease and the boys are."

Chapter 10

Chasing Shadows

January 2032

Casey looked everywhere he could think for Teresa and the boys. It was a cold Wednesday afternoon, so he called her office in the capital and talked to her boss, he went to the grocery store, the beauty shop, the mall, the shoe store and the clothing store that she usually frequents.

Casey submitted a missing persons report with the Carson City police and the Nevada State Patrol. The next day he went to see Governor Martin Gonzalez and Teresa's co-workers.

He found out that there was another person missing from the Capital workforce and the same shadows were on his garage door and driveway.

Casey met Martin in the hall and they talked about the man who had been reported missing yesterday.

"I saw an article in the newspaper about shadows in Dallas and how someone from NASA was there examining the shadows." Martin said.

"Hey! That's a good idea." Casey said. "May I use your phone, sir?"

"Sure go right ahead." Martin said indicating the phone on the desk.

Casey dialed the number Chuck had given to him the last time they were together.

"NASA Labs, this is Chuck. May I help you?"

"Chuck, this is Casey. Are you guys familiar with these shadows?"

"Yeah, sort of."

"I need you to get over here right away. Tease is missing and there's a shadow on my front porch and I've got a bad feeling about this. Bring anyone you can who can provide some help and there is at least one other missing person who works in the State Capital. Hurry."

"I'll be there tomorrow, Case."

Chuck and the other three arrived at eleven thirty the next day. Governor Gonzalez and Casey were there to meet them at the airport.

Coolie explained everything to both of them on the ride back to the Governors office.

"You mean there's some maniac out there killing people with this machine of yours?" Casey screamed.

"Casey. Listen." Coolie said. "These people aren't dead."

"What? Well, then, where is she?"

"I don't know." Coolie said.

"How do we find her?"

"I don't know, but we're working on it."

"Then work a little harder!" Casey's voice began to get louder each time he spoke.

"We are arriving at the Capital Office Building, Governor." The chauffeur said leaning back toward them.

It was all they could do to contain Casey during the walk into the Capital offices.

"Close the door tightly so no one will hear us. No sense adding to the panic."

"The machine, Spector, that was stolen was a time travel machine. The people affected by the machine are not dead, they have been sent to another time." Coolie said.

"OK. I can live with that. What time are they living in?" Casey asked.

"I don't know."

"Then how do we find them?"

"I don't know."

"You're a lot of help." Casey was raising his voice again.

Chuck and Bruce took Casey out onto the hall and calmed him down again.

"Listen Casey. We need all the help we can get. Why don't you come to work with us and together we can find the answer to this puzzle."

"OK. You get me the transfer, and I'll come to NASA with you and I'll work my butt off. But I'm not going to stop or calm down until I get Tease back and this maniac is stopped."

Later that afternoon Coolie and Casey examined the shadows on the front porch at Casey's house and later the garage door and driveway of Juan Fernandez. Coolie produced his new Thetiameter from his toolbox and began to scan the shadow for radiation.

"The level of radioactivity is extremely low here, nearly non-existent, I wonder why. Each of the other shadows we have examined have had a lot of this strange new particle in them."

"What new particle?" Casey asked.

"It's the Theta particle, I have never seen it before." Coolie said.

"Maybe some other scientist has run across it."

"That's a great idea. We had better get back to the lab. Let's go examine that other shadow, then I need to make some calls. Let's get going."

They worked all afternoon at the two houses and when all the information had been written, they were on their way.

"Expect your orders in a few days Casey. I'll send them to your Governor." Chuck said.

By the time Casey flew the Mirage back to Monterrey the next day, Governor Pete had already heard about Teresa and the transfer. Casey left for NASA on the following Friday.

"I'm sorry to see you leave this way, Casey, but I think you're just the man to fix this craziness that's going on. I'm proud to call you a friend." Pete said.

Both men shook hands and talked like old friends about to go off to war for several minutes before Casey left.

Mitchell called all twenty-four of his men in from the field for a good old heart to heart talk. The trouble was, Mitchell did all the talking.

"You idiots! I told you to do it quietly! There is some idiot television newsman telling everyone in the country there are aliens kidnapping people! It's all over the news! I said quietly! That's what I meant!"

Mitchell was screaming at the top of his lungs. Mitchell could be unpleasant when he wanted to be, and he really wanted to be now.

"One more screw-up and all of you will be purified and I'll find someone who will follow my orders! From now on, you will report to me every day by phone! Each one of you! Now get out of here! And go to different places, I don't want any of this to be traced back to any of you, or me!"

The shadows in the cities and towns across America stopped as mysteriously as they started, however, shadows have been appearing in out of the way places. The media hasn't picked up on this as yet.

The shadows are only being seen in the most out of the way places, like on the side of a road or highway, or a railroad track, or in open fields and meadows where no one would look. The shadow troops have taught themselves how use the camera quietly and surreptitiously. Around the country, the shadows are going undetected now.

"What I want to know is this. How do I fit in with this 'Spector' and space stuff that you're talking about, and how do we all come together?" Casey asked.

Bruce and Chuck began to explain space and time.

"Wait a minute. I spent four years studying all this, I understand the basics of Astrophysics and space and time. I want to know the specifics of how I fit into your crazy scheme."

Casey's attitude wasn't getting any better.

"We want you to fly the space shuttle through space and time and record every item you might see, hear and experience. We will install video cameras and audio microphones to capture everything. We will chart a course for you to travel to get the most benefit from this flight." Coolie said.

Coolie always finds a way to step in and calm the situation down. He should have been a diplomat.

"But I can't fly through time. Nobody can."

The Spector Team, Bruce, Chuck, Ken and Dr. Kuhlmann explained every detail of the proposed experiment to Casey.

"There are some very special points I want you to try. I'll go over them with you as soon as I can formulate them in my mind and put them down on paper and we will go over them completely."

Coolie spent a lot of time calibrating his Thetiacmeter to measure the sample strength in a scale of one to one hundred units, and writing operating and calibrating instructions for the other four men. He sent them out in pairs to investigate the shadows and collect samples, take precise measurements of Theta strength, draw shapes and measure sizes.

Casey and Chuck traveled to Oklahoma City to photograph, measure in feet and inches, draw pictures and take radioactive samples of the shadows on Reno Street.

Bruce and Ken started in New Orleans on Rampart and Lafayette Streets to accomplish the same tasks that Coolie had so meticulously drawn out for the field teams. Each of them had a list of cities and towns to visit and glean every scrap of information they could from townspeople, police and citizens who might have seen something.

"Hey Chuck, how are you and Yvonne getting along? It must be tough being out here with me while she is back in Redlake cooling her heels."

"Yeah, and I'll be glad to find some reason to go to Coolie's place as soon as we get done with this trip, too. You're a good friend, but she is a whole lot better looking than you, and a lot more fun."

"I'm hurt." Casey feigned pain and a hurt expression.

The Team has decided to gather missing person reports from all around the country and code the information and feed the data into a central database just for this sort of use.

"Then we'll sort out the shadows and make a separate database of that. Maybe there will be some common denominator when we match the information together."

NASA has plenty of data processing personnel to build and maintain the database. The programmers have been working on this little project for six months and are only now beginning to see the light at the end of the tunnel. The program will be fully functional in another month or two.

Meanwhile, it took Coolie and his team months to isolate Theta from the rest of the specimens. He gathered many bags of material from the mysterious shadows in all kinds of containers, then he had to sort through each and every one of them.

He did finally separate one hundred potent Theta particles into a nice little special container where he could study them without any outside interference from other sources.

Coolie did experiments with mice, rabbits, cats and dogs, all with the same results. Theta will cure the animals of any virus that could be injected into them.

The biggest discovery that Coolie made during those long months was that the animals all exhibited a rage if they had a virus, and no rage if they did not. It didn't seem to matter how much Theta was on them, if there was no virus, then no symptoms of rage were observed.

The team mapped the data from the shadows and missing persons reports and the two reports coincided with streaks moving northward from the southwest where the waters flooded the desert. The mapping procedure provided lines toward Canada and one definite line across the southern coast where it stopped in Alabama.

"You know, I think we should call ourselves 'The Shadow Team'." They all had a good laugh at that.

"Right, and wear hoods and capes too."

Ken Hiroshi was watching TV one afternoon when the Wally Wilson Show came on the channel.

"Where do they get these guys? Hey Bruce, come see this."

One of those super-sensational television talk show hosts who always puts the most idiotic people and news on their show has another unbelievable guest with as unbelievable story as any heard on TV in the last several years.

"It's the Wally Wilson Show from Los Angeles with a man who is promoting the premise that the end of the world has finally come, because, as he said, 'The proof is in the shadows.'"

"My guest today is Herbert Morton, who says that he saw the person, or being, that has made the shadows around the country over the past several months."

The camera panned around the audience and came to rest on Wallace "Wally" Wilson, the host, and the man seated next to him.

"Herb, what was it that you say you saw out there?"

"It was the devil! I'm telling you that I saw the devil! All in red with horns and breathing fire."

"You saw the devil? Dressed in red with horns and everything? Is that what you're telling us?"

"Not dressed in red, he had red skin, not red clothes. He had horns and a pointed tongue and he breathed fire on these people and there was a real bright flash and they all disappeared. He sent them to Hell."

"Where did he go after this all happened, Herb?"

"The devil has come for his due, the shadows are all that's left from the ones he has taken to Hell with him. And that's all that I know."

Herb was convinced that he had seen the devil and that there would soon be Hell on earth. He was close.

Bruce and Ken watched with the scientific curiosity of one who has found a long sought answer.

"There's the guy with our Spector, let's go."

"Remember, we're looking for a guy in a red coat with the Spector somewhere in LA, but we'll have to interview this nut Morton to get the location of the shadows."

After a couple of days of travel to Los Angeles, listening to the deranged ramblings of Herb Morton and searching the area and finding the shadows, Bruce and Ken collapsed on the motel bed and switched on the TV for some entertainment and relaxation. A local news reporter was telling about shadows found in Huntsville just last night.

"They couldn't have been the same guy, someone has built more of these and is using them as weapons. We've got a big problem!"

The government decided to make the Northwest Territories and Greenland into giant Indian reservations. All Indians who were found by the government wandering the countryside were shipped to one of these two locations. The only good thing about it from the Indian's point of view, was that they would have free run of the whole area.

After the flood, all of the Indian tribes living in the area were forced to vacate in the face of the advancing water. Word was passed around the southwestern tribes about the MacKenzie mountains and river and all the tribes decided to go there.

The Indians moved north in small groups, all the other people ran for the cities. A sense of panic washed all across the area with people moving and running, and shadows following the tribes northward.

It was a long summer. First they ran from the flood, then the shadows, then the winter snow. Teresa's tribal family made it to the land that Casey had told them about and they found places to build houses and caves to live in. There were many caves and canyons in the foothills between the MacKenzie river and the MacKenzie mountains.

During the migration, one Zuni Indian man, Elia, saw two men with a camera stop some of the tribe traveling near them as they were crossing Colorado.

"What did you see Elia?"

"The two men set up their camera to take a picture and there was a bright flash and all of our people were gone, Chief."

"Pass the word to all the tribal peoples to watch out for men with cameras. Do not allow any pictures to be taken and do not allow anyone with a camera near the tribes."

"How are you and Yvonne getting along, Chuck?" Casey asked.

"I have been flying back to see Yvonne every month since the beginning."

"Sounds like you're getting serious, man."

"She's really a wonderful woman and she makes me feel good, what more could I ask?" Chuck said.

"How far are you going to go with this?"

"As far as she'll let me."

The Shadow Team was hard at work. Bags of material were swept from the ground and buildings at the point of every investigation of the shadows. They were analyzed for everything the NASA Team could think of. They found the Theta particles in the shadows, but not much more. Coolie made sure to count parts per million of Theta and record every detail. He determined that the particles were carried on the people who were purified.

"I wonder if there is any value to the Theta particles?"

"You know, I was sick when that comet came over and didn't get out of the house for days." Casey said.

Coolie used his Thetiacmeter to measure the Theta particles on Casey.

"I have a reading of twenty four from you Casey, almost the same as Teresa's shadow. It read eighteen. This certainly brings up an interesting postulate. You know that I worked with the animals we have at the lab, and recorded all the results, but I had no idea that it could be converted to human behavior as well.

"I have an idea. Why don't we find someone who exhibits the rage syndrome and see if we can remove it from them?"

It wasn't hard for the Team to find someone in one of the hospitals who was infected with HIV. The man was brought back to the lab and Coolie treated him with one hundred parts per million of Theta particles for the next few weeks. The man was watched very carefully and every detail was carefully recorded.

Just as they had hoped and Coolie had predicted, the man developed an anger, then he became mad at everything around him and finally the rage took over. The rage held him in its grip for twenty three days and subsided, during which time he was kept in a cell for everyone's protection.

Once the rage had left the man, the doctors tested him for the HIV virus. No sign of the virus could be found.

"Now we need to do one more test to confirm my findings."

"What is the next test?"

"We will find someone with the rage and send him ahead in time for a minute or two to observe if the rage has left him."

"That's ridiculous, you can't do that." Casey said.

Coolie put out the word to the Houston Police to bring the man who was exhibiting the rage to him immediately. It was only a few days before the Police called with a man in handcuffs, and brought him to the lab.

"Bruce will you set up the equipment?"

"Casey and Chuck, will you place the subject in the chair?"

"Officers will you wait out in the hall with Ken here?"

"Alright sir, please put these dark glasses on and sit very still for me. Thank you."

FLASH!

The man disappeared, and while he was gone they swept up the shadow from under him and tested it for Theta.

"One hundred fifty parts per million."

One minute and twenty seconds later, the man appeared looking quite disconnected from reality. They hurried to measure Theta on him before the officers were returned to the lab.

"One part per million. That's the way I like an experiment to work, very exact. I think we have it."

Chapter 11

The Dome

January 2033

The political campaign of '33 would soon be a shock to many around the country, but more of a shock to the residents of the State of Arizona. Jolly and Billy contacted Mitchell by phone just after New Years and later in February in person at his office.

"We think you should run for US Senator, Mitch. We will help you all the way." Jolly said.

"Let's get an election committee and some kind of an organization together." Billy said.

"The Indian purification is continuing quietly all through the country by your followers. We have several of our guys working in the south and southwest, with one pair of loyal workers following the Indians on their migration north."

"Now it's time for you to become a 'Man of the People' and grab as much power as you can. Besides, the purification can be speeded up after you are elected."

The computer gurus at NASA cranked up their program and fed all the missing persons information and all the reported "shadow" sightings into the computer. The computer has displayed a large map of the US with all the information thereon.

"Look at this guys. It looks like the point of origin is Lake Mojave and everything radiates out from it. The spots on the map seem to be making lines along the coast through Texas and toward Alabama, where they stop." Chuck said.

"These lines are running north through Nevada and Colorado, across Montana and the Dakotas into the Canadian states." Ken said.

"And on into an area near the MacKenzie River." Casey finished Ken's sentence from across the room. "Come on, we're going to go hunting for shadows."

Sakima and his betrothed Aquene, a name meaning peace, were two of the Indians who had been uprooted from their homes in southern California and Arizona at the time of the great flood, have traveled with their families the huge distance to the cold north country of the Northwest Territories. They were away from the settlement on horseback hunting for food, when they saw an unusually bright flash in the woods ahead. Two of the shadow troops had purified six Indians in the snow right before their eyes.

"Aquene, you take the one in the open." He said and he spurred his horse into a gallop.

The two of them approached the two shadow troops and when the man with the camera swung it around toward them, Sakima and Aquene shot and killed them both.

"We will take everything back to the settlement to show the council."

Sakima and Aquene gathered up every little scrap they could find in the snow and packed it all into the nearby four wheel drive pickup truck the two were driving. He marked the trees for a sign in case they had to return to the place at another time.

"Grandfather, we saw these two men shoot our brothers with a bright flash from their camera and our brothers all disappeared. We killed both men and we have brought the bodies and their truck."

"You have done well, my child. Please unload all their belongings into the council tent and hide the truck in a cave in the mountains there." Judge pointed toward the cliffs as he spoke to them.

Aquene and her fiancé did as they were told and unloaded every little scrap into the tent, then they hid the truck in a nearby cave for future use.

"Daniel, get someone to pack these bodies into snow and ice to preserve them. I need to contact someone for help." Judge said.

Meanwhile Casey and his friends were trucking their way northward into the Canadian states and on toward the MacKenzie river. It was a long hard drive through the Dakotas and the dirt roads of Saskatchewan, but it got much worse when the roads became non-existent in the Northwest Territory.

They had been driving a large six door van with all the accommodations that were available, but all five of them were exhausted when they stepped out into the cold Canadian air in the MacKenzie Mountain Range. Many of the residents came out to meet the van as Casey and the NASA team drove into the tiny town. The first person to recognize them was the Judge himself.

"Casey, could you come here, we have something to show you, bring your scientist friends, this might be important." Judge said.

Judge explained what happened to Casey and the Team as they walked to the ice pack where the bodies were stored. Once the bodies were uncovered, Bruce and Chuck began to inspect them for any indications of their identity and other telltale signs.

"We have their weapon and their personal items in the Council tent."

"What is this around his neck?" Bruce said.

He held up a gold chain with a small gold rounded square pendant with a design painted in red on it. It was a foreshortened cross of red with rounded edges inside a circle of white. Bruce handed the pendant to Chuck, who examined it and passed it on to Coolie. It made the rounds to everyone standing there in the group.

"Are we all agreed?" Chuck asked.

"Yes, it is definitely a Klan symbol. I can see that they are pursuing the Indians." Casey said.

"I told you we were followed." Sakima said.

"We must do something."

"We must find a way to hide our people." Judge said.

"I have an idea, sir." Elia Payat said.

Elia was an engineer and inventor, and regularly solved the problems of the various tribes when they were living back home in Arizona. He explained his idea there in the snow and all of them agreed to proceed with the plan.

"Chuck, Let's look at their personal effects, maybe we can find out who they were and who they were working for." Coolie said.

The Arizona Democratic State Assembly was held on the first Saturday of May, and Representative Charles Casado nominated Mitchell Cordel for US Senator from Arizona. Mitchell gave a rousing speech about better living conditions and the crowd sat quietly as he finished and walked off the platform. What they didn't know was, the better living conditions that Mitchell was talking about meant better for him. Mitchell barely made the ballot for the primary.

"How is the purification coming along?" Mitchell asked.

"Slowly and quietly. Although I haven't heard from the team in the Canadian states lately."

"Good, but check on them."

Mitchell is now on the ballot with one other man, Representative Rodgers from Flagstaff, and the primary election to determine the party's candidate will be in August. You can bet Mitchell will be running hard this time.

Elia described his idea to the Team from NASA and they agreed in principle with it, but the practical matters concerning building a gigantic plastic dome big enough to cover a small town were enough to make all of them feel sick.

A company named Royal Plastics in Pennsylvania has been experimenting with a new technique. Elia and two of his engineering friends have set off to Pennsylvania for more information and study.

It was a long hard drive across the country from their little town just south of the Arctic Circle back to civilization and Pennsylvania. Royal Plastics was glad to train the three men in the new technique and sell them all the tools and materials they would need for the first project.

Royal Plastics was happy to show the delegation of engineers around their plant and offices. Explanations and discussions concerning the new plastic and the new technique lasted four days, but finally the training was finished.

Payment was made and Elia and the others were on their way back to their new adopted home driving the confiscated pickup truck loaded with their purchase. It would be three or four weeks before everything would be delivered, but that would give the Indians time to prepare the site for the coming technology.

Since the towns were not yet built, Elia and his crew picked a site and began to prepare it for the plastic dome that was to be installed. The new technique that Royal developed was to spray the specially developed plastic into the air from a special ring which had been fitted with spray orifices while air is blown up to support the dome as it hardened in place. It only took two weeks for the equipment to be set into place and the dome blown into shape.

The dome was made from one large piece of unbreakable plastic and was clear enough to see through, but if they could see out, then others could see in as well.

"Elia, I see only two problems." Judge said. "How do we move our people in and out of our towns inside these domes and how do we hide them?"

"I have answers for both of your questions. Some years ago I was working on another problem and stumbled onto the answer, but it was of no use until now. We will need one of those engines from the Commutercopter, I have called the inventor and he is on his way here. I have all the other materials. In answer to the first question, we can make tunnels from those nearby rocks to the town sites and our entrances will be unseen and guarded."

A Council meeting was held where Elia explained in great detail how he would protect the domes and where to dig the tunnels leading to the domes. Soon everyone was digging tunnels and shoring them up with timbers from the nearby forests.

Inside the glass-domed city, a projector shows a continuous picture of the outside terrain onto the inside of the glass dome. Elia put together a series of lenses and projection equipment to produce an illusion for the passers-by. From the outside it just looks like everything else around, you could ride or fly past the dome and never notice it.

Fred Goss was happy to help with the dome project and be working with his friends again.

"I have changed the engine from the Commutercopter to power our shroud. It will use the water from the MacKenzie River and special additives to afford proper operation." Fred said.

"That's the name, Shroud."

"There's no place like dome."

"I knew someone would say that."

"Now that we have a safe and secure place, Judge, May I and my team use space here for our lab? There are many questions for which we must find answers and we cannot afford interruptions or leaks." Coolie asked.

"We will all help you with your mission." Judge said.

The Council decided to post a guard at the entrance to the tunnel in the rocks. All others would work on houses inside the dome for all who lived there. The lab will be a separate building of adobe in the center of the dome. The shroud must be cared for by technical people as well.

Judge and the Council had given the team access to a building in the center of the dome until more space was available for the research facility. All of the members of the team knew that they had no time to lose to find the answers to these very difficult questions.

"Let's review what we know aloud and maybe we can brainstorm an answer. I'll start. We know that the particle called Theta from the comet is what is producing the rage in people." Coolie said.

"We know that only people who are sick are affected by the particle. We know that the particle will cure all viruses, but causes aggression as the virus is being cured including the common cold. We know that if the dose is less than 100 parts per million, no effects are seen." Bruce said.

"We don't know what their dangers and the values are but this rage thing is pretty obvious but we don't know why it doesn't effect some people, we need to test more. Tests were run on the theta particles and we found that the particles cause rage in all animals when the dose is more than 100 parts per million." Chuck said.

"We know that someone has stolen Spector and has reproduced it and is shooting people with it. We know that we have captured one of the reproduced cameras from the two men who were shot in the forest." Coolie said.

"We know that when a person is shot with the camera, the particles are left behind in their shadow." Bruce said.

"We know that these two men were wearing Klan symbols, and hunting these tribes with their camera." Chuck said.

"We know that the place of origin of the shadows was somewhere in the Arizona desert. Who could have possibly done this?" Coolie asked.

Casey was only partially listening until the last few ideas were spoken.

"Mitchell! Mitchell could have done this!" Casey said. "And if I find out that he's the one responsible for my Teresa's death, I'll kill him with my bare hands, and then I'll shoot him!"

Casey was suddenly seething with anger. Bruce and Chuck went to him to try to calm him down. Casey was not someone you wanted to be around when he was this angry.

Fred had been just sitting and listening to the brainstorming.

"You don't mean that kid from Phoenix who you were always fighting with, do you?" Fred said.

"The very same."

Mitchell was very busy making speeches, shaking hands and making himself sick being around the common people. He has never thought of himself as one of them. Mitchell has always thought of himself as 'special'.

"I just can't keep this up! Do you realize that I am shaking hands with Indians and Mexicans! I don't even like looking at them, and you have me shaking their hands!" Mitchell said.

"How do you expect to get yourself elected if we don't portray you as a friend of the people? What's the matter with you? Now get out there and give your speech on retirement." Carlos said.

Mitchell's speech on retirement was prepared by his speech writer and given with as much emotion as the lip service he performed during one of his handshaking sessions outside the gates of one of the many State Government facilities.

What were Mitchell's real feelings about retirement? That's an easy one to answer and I quote, "If you are purified, don't worry about it, you won't be around to collect your retirement."

Two more domes are being built and additional tunnels are being dug to connect all three together. The center dome will be devoted exclusively to the research team and those who will be working with them.

Once the third dome was built, guards were posted at each of the entrances in the rocks on eight hour shifts around the clock. No sense taking any more chances.

It took Mitchell a little time to get revved up for the campaign trail, but once he built up a full head of steam, he seemed unstoppable. His speech on pollution was better than his last. He didn't sound quite as glib and insincere, and although the crowds weren't cheering, they weren't booing anymore.

Of course, the crowds don't have the slightest inkling what he had in mind or what he means when he says something. Being against pollution means, "The purified won't pollute, so let's hurry the purification along."

Ken made a mammoth discovery while working in the lab in Houston. He immediately placed a phone call to the lab in the dome to Coolie to explain what he had found. Coolie put Ken on the vidphone for a conference call.

"Something is not in phase with everything else and I think the victims have jumped across the timeline to another timeline, but I don't know how that is possible. The first Spector had something wrong with it that could have caused the jump between timelines. I think the particles don't belong on the other side and they make the person see into the other timeline and their mind can't handle it, therefore the rage." Ken said.

"That is astounding Ken." Coolie said.

"We need a test to prove it, it has locked something out of phase and I'm not sure what we will find." Ken said.

"We can't test it with someone unless we send another Spector and a memory module back with them so they can get back and tell us what they find. We must build two with the backwards part, one for the lab and one for the subject." Bruce said.

"But first we must figure out how to send both the subject and the camera back together." Chuck always was the sensitive one in the crowd.

"Chuck, would you go back to the lab and help Ken with that little detail? We really need to know how to solve that if we are to succeed with this." Coolie said.

"Now then, the four of us have a very important experiment to complete. One of you must go back in time with the memory module and spend some time there and return. We know that you can put the memory module under your clothing and it will stay with you. Today is August tenth, I will set the Automatic Return sequence for August seventeenth, when you will return here." Coolie said.

Casey and Bruce stood there with a look of amazement on their faces.

"Who wants to go?"

"Casey does." Bruce said.

"No, Bruce. You're unattached, you're the one. Come over here I want to tell you what you are to do. Now listen carefully." Coolie said.

Coolie and Bruce huddled at the desk for nearly an hour in preparation to this first monumental experiment. Finally Bruce took his place in the room in front of the Spector.

"OK, I'm ready."

FLASH!

An instant later Bruce was sitting at his desk in the lab at NASA as a voice played into his earphone from the memory module.

"Hello Bruce, this is Casey. You have been sent back from our time to find out where you are right now. As you get answers, speak them into the microphone attached to your headset. There is a push to talk switch on the side of your headset as well. Don't forget, you must write everything on the pad in your inside pocket for us to read once you return here to us. See you soon."

Bruce went about completing the tasks that Casey was telling to him over his memory module. Once Bruce got settled into the routine of his assignment, he began to enjoy it. The year was 1961 and NASA was involved in a very unique space mission during the week that Bruce spent in Houston.

The primary election came and went on a seemingly quiet day in August without much fan fare except what the political parties and the candidates could muster.

Mitchell won the primary election from his opponent by one percent of the vote. Representative Rodgers ran hard but Mitchell's campaign organization overwhelmed him with half-truths and innuendoes. Rodgers gave his consolation speech just before dinner on that election day.

It was five minutes after one in the afternoon of August seventeenth when Bruce appeared in the middle of the lab in the dome.

"It worked! It worked!" Coolie said.

Coolie was jumping around like a kid of ten. "Tell us all about it, Bruce, quickly."

It was March when Chuck left the dome to return to Houston to help Ken find the answers to the questions. This was important and they all knew it, but it was beginning to drag them all down. Chuck hadn't seen Yvonne since the New Years party in Redlake and he missed her more than he could say.

It was the tenth of October when Ken and Chuck found the answer. Ten minutes later Chuck was on the phone to Redlake.

"Yvonne, I love you and I can't live without you, will you marry me and come to the most amazing dome you have ever seen and live there with me?"

"Where is this amazing dome, Chuck honey?"

"In the MacKenzie Mountains next to the MacKenzie River. You should love it after living in Frozenfeet, Minnesota." Chuck said.

"Alright, I'll be ready to go when you get here. Bye, lover."

"Who ever stole Spector didn't get the memory module, it was in Redlake and without the memory module the person sent back in time won't know who, where or what they are."

"That's it!"

"I know where they are! Coolie screamed. "Ken was right! All the pieces fit!"

He stood there with that look of smug satisfaction that you get when you have just figured something out right in front of all the smart guys who were working on it before you started.

"OK, are you going to tell us or are we going to have to beat it out of you?" Casey said. The others laughed at Casey's impatience.

"Let's find a board that I can work on."

Coolie strode to the board as if he owned the world and took one of the colored markers. He meticulously worked at the board and told the others the details of the out of phase transfer. Each time he indicated an item he needed, they jumped when he spoke and delivered. It wasn't long before the board looked like something out an old movie showing Einstein and his theories.

"Look, Coolie. All this stuff doesn't explain what we have to do and how we do it."

"Ah, but it does. Don't you see this? These formulas will allow me to send one of you back to the exact day we choose to accomplish any feat we need." Coolie said.

"I want to see Teresa!"

"You will, my boy. You will."

The General Election around the country in November held many surprises for people in every state. Law and Order was the main theme that won elections for candidates, and Mitchell was no exception.

Mitchell lied through his teeth during every speech and social gathering, but he said what the voters wanted to hear and they rewarded him with the seat in the US Senate which he was vying for.

It was admittedly, the smallest margin ever to carry the election in the history of the State of Arizona, but as someone once said, "It only takes one vote to win".

Chapter 12
The Purification Continues

January 2034

Television reception from the domes has been difficult to achieve, but with a fount of scientific minds working in the lab, this task was not one of great concern to them. Now the people living in the domes have news and entertainment in many languages from Europe, Asia and North America.

Reports of shadows from around the United States are a daily occurrence on US television and radio news now, with many varied groups talking about the end of the world.

The Christians are talking about God and his wrath ending the world and the atheists are talking about the devil taking over the world. Scientists are talking about errant celestial bodies crashing into the earth, and just plain crazies are talking about anything and everything that will attract attention to them. It seems like all manner of fanatics have crawled out of the woodwork to appear on any TV talk show that will oblige them.

There always seems to be an "eyewitness" to these ludicrous happenings, these eyewitnesses will make up any kind of story if it will get them on TV. They will say they saw it just to say it and they seem to

195

receive some perverse reflected glory from someone else's misfortune.

During the three weeks following the completion of the installation of the antenna system for the domes, Bruce, Casey, Coolie and Fred watched as reports of all kinds of sightings by these eyewitnesses were made on national TV. There was one man who saw the devil and demons carrying people away, another saw a poltergeist eating people whole.

A group of women swore they saw an alien invasion with UFOs transporting people up into the spacecraft. Two kids said they saw subterranean creatures devouring whole houses and buildings and a mailman said he saw two little green men with big heads shoot a group of people with their ray gun and they all disappeared.

By far the funniest story was told by a supposedly reputable source, Dr. David Logan, who tried to convince a TV talk show host that sunspots were the reason for the shadows.

The most pathetic thing about the whole unbelievable scenario unfolded on daytime television, is the ones who watch these shows and believe the lies - stories - told by the eye witnesses who fabricated these ridiculous stories.

"I've noticed there's one little detail that the news has never reported that shadows have been found anywhere in the world except North America." Fred said.

"Ya know, you're right. I wonder why we haven't heard of any shadows appearing from any other country in the world." Casey said.

Mitchell campaigned long and hard for the seat of US Senator from Arizona. He had help from Casado, Nash and Rodgers, but hardly anyone else. The margin of the win was meager, but Mitchell will tell all who will listen that he was given a mandate by the people to right the wrongs of the world.

"Nice office."

"Thanks, come on in." Mitchell said.

Bobby Nash, Jolly Rodgers and Chuck Casado followed Mitchell into the huge office. The walls were covered with expensive wood and shelves and pictures of former Senators. A huge oak desk dominated the room with an equally large black leather swivel chair behind it.

Mitchell took a seat in the black chair and indicated to his comrades to find a seat in one of the leather covered chairs beside and in front of the desk.

"I have decided that the four larger Caribbean Islands would make wonderful resorts for the better people of this country, and therefore I want these lands to be purified first. All whites must be removed first, in order that they do not see or know what is happening there." Mitchell said.

"After the natives are removed, we will capture all the land and later sell it to US companies for hotels, resorts, airports and anything else we can think of." Bobby said.

"Great idea, Bobby. We also might want to reserve a special plot of land for ourselves to use as a private hideaway." Jolly said.

"Of course, we will select the best, most beautiful section of the islands." Bobby said.

"You two are thinking so small. Why not have a special place on each of the islands? Ha, ha, ha." Mitchell said.

Bobby was on the phone sending out the call for all their troops to report to Bobby at his office in Birmingham as soon as possible.

"Send all the troops to the islands and have them post signs for all whites to evacuate the islands. Tell them anything you want. Tell them the government needs them back home. I don't care what you tell them, just do it!" Mitchell said.

"Do it slowly and quietly so that the media doesn't get suspicious. Start with the smaller islands. Jolly, will you write the signs and get them printed and distributed to the troops?" Mitchell said.

"Sure Mitchell."

"Send someone to survey each island for the best parcel of land and mark it for us." Mitchell said.

From the beginning, Fred and Elia knew that the Shroud was the solution to disguising the domes. They also knew that the Commutercopter engine was just the thing to supply the power for the mechanism, but exhaust was always a problem. The exhaust couldn't be piped into the outside air. That would be a dead giveaway.

"What do we do?" Fred asked.

"Let's run a pipe underground and away from the domes." Elia said.

"Still see the smoke."

"You got a better idea?"

"Let's run the pipe into the river. Then even if some steam rises, it'll look natural."

Every Tuesday afternoon, the lab dwellers attend their strategy meeting to brainstorm problems and answer questions regarding the portion of the project they happen to be working on at that particular time.

Chuck and Ken participate in this function by way of vidphone. From the beginning, Coolie has been working on the problem of the backwards parts, Theta and the rage. Coolie stood up and went to the board.

"I believe that I know how to add the date and time to the Spector." Coolie said.

"That's great." Fred said.

"I also think that I am close to pinpointing the destination location as well."

"That's even better!" Casey exclaimed. "What about the other timeline?"

"But we don't know how to get there yet." Coolie said.

"Yes we do." Said Ken from the vidphone. "We can't cross to the other side and go back on this side or the other side at the same time, but Chuck has figured out how to cross to the other side. We could do that today. We're not quite sure how to come back yet."

"Count me in! When can I go see Teresa? I don't care about coming back, I want to be where she is." Casey said.

Both teams worked feverishly to find the answers to how to return to the present, and late in March,

Chuck and Ken, working in the lab in Houston finished the design to add the destination, date and time to the Spector. They can now send someone to the exact time and place chosen.

"We have found evidence that there is another parallel time line and that we shouldn't be here. We believe that all of those missing people are there, wherever there is." Ken said.

"How far can we go into the past and still come back? Five, ten, fifteen, twenty years?" Fred asked.

"We don't know yet, maybe indefinite." Ken said.

"Let's try a hundred years." Coolie said.

"Can we get back if we are not at the exact spot that we left?" Casey asked.

"Yes, I will set all that from the settings here and you will have the AR button with you." Coolie said.

"Where do we want to go?" Chuck asked.

"Since I'm the guinea pig, I would like to see that first flight at Kitty Hawk." Bruce said.

The Team worked to make everything ready for Bruce's trip to North Carolina. Bruce was excited that he would be able to witness this historical event.

"I've made three controls for the Spector here in the lab. They are this selector for Future and Past, this Auto Return switch, the auto return is a very important part of this machine, and the destination panel. Prior to the trip, we will set these controls to the date and time of your arrival here on these controls, and the duration of stay here, and most important, we must set the place where you will return here on this panel." Coolie said.

Coolie pointed out each control to Bruce as he spoke. "The red button here on the side will begin the firing sequence."

Everything was ready, the controls were set and Bruce took his place in the middle of the room.

FLASH!

Bruce found himself standing in a back alley and looked around at the unusual surroundings. Casey's voice spoke to him through the earphone and Bruce did as he was instructed. He retrieved the pad of paper and pencil from his inside coat pocket and walked to the street and turned on his voice-activated recorder. There was a general store just two blocks down the street and Bruce walked the wooden sidewalks to the store.

"Good afternoon, young man. How are you?" The proprietor said.

"Fine thank you sir. Do you have a newspaper?" Bruce asked.

"Sure thing. I have yesterdays here, I've already read it so just take it with you."

Bruce read the date from the top of the page.

"December 15th, 1903. Kitty Hawk, North Carolina. Where might I find a ride to Kill Devil Hills and a room for the night, sir?" Bruce asked.

"Well son, the room is easy. Right across the street to the hotel. About the ride, I could let you have my buggy out back, but my horse is down at the livery, and you'll have to take care of her yourself. You think you want to do that?"

"Yes sir, and I'll be happy to pay you a fair price for the use of it too."

Bruce walked across the street and registered for his room. He then visited the livery to find the horse. The man at the livery told Bruce that all the tack was hanging on the sides of the stall and he helped get the horse ready for the ride south down the beaches of Bodie Island.

Bruce drove the buggy with great anticipation along the water. Soon he saw a group of buildings and several men standing around. It was a blustery and cold day, not as cold as Redlake or MacKenzie, but it was December and cold. The wind was blowing hard and it felt as if the cold was blowing right through him.

The men stopped talking as he drove up.

"Hi, I'm Bruce. Are you going to fly today?"

"No, not today. It is far too windy, we have already closed the barn where the flyer is housed."

"May I see it, sir?" Bruce asked.

"Just Wilbur, not sir, and yes come on in here with me."

Bruce followed Wilbur into the barn and gasped as he looked at The Wright Flyer. It seemed much bigger to him than he thought it would be, although he had only seen pictures of it. Bruce ran his hands over the wings and the struts and the tail, it was amazing. He was actually touching the first airplane before it had ever been flown.

"When will you fly it, Wilbur?"

"We think the storms will calm by morning. Orville and I hope to try again then. Will we see you again, Bruce?"

"Oh yes! Nothing could stop me from witnessing this event."

December 17th, 1903 was a very busy day for Bruce. He didn't sleep much that night and he was in the buggy heading for the beach long before eight a.m. Before the day was over, Bruce witnessed Wilbur and Orville make four historic flights.

The longest was eight hundred fifty two feet. But now the day was done and Bruce had to go to his room and find the Auto Return switch and go back to his own time, over a hundred years into the future. There was a part of him that wanted to stay here with Wilbur and Orville, but there was much work to be done.

A second later Bruce was standing in the lab dome and nearly no one noticed him appear. After a few minutes, Fred noticed him and helped him find a chair. Soon all of them were hovering around Bruce and asking questions. Spector was a success.

Late in April, in the state of Pacifica where no one had thought to look before, Marcos Bearga, a farmer and his son, Diego, were searching desperately for water for their crops and animals. They had enlisted the aid of Angel Fernandez, a kind of local hero and seer, to help with his dousing stick from the nearest town, El Arco. The three of them decided the best place to begin the search for the elusive water was in a low flat area in the Vizcaino Desert in the middle of the peninsula.

They had searched for more than two months with the dousing stick bending down several times each day, but when their borrowed drilling equipment was brought to bear, the search was fruitless. Finally in desperation, the three exhausted men each threw a rock into the air and the drill was pointed to the center of the triangle where they landed. After an hour of drilling, a telltale noise was heard from the machinery, then from the ground came the same noises.

"Stop! Marcos! Stop!" Angel yelled.

"What? Why do you say stop?"

"If we continue to drill we will have oil all over the sand." Angel said.

"But Angel, we are drilling for water." Marcos said.

"Those noises we are hearing now are noises from the oil releasing to the surface." Angel said.

"What shall we do?" Diego asked.

"We must hurry to the state offices and file our claim on this land. You remember that we have heard that the state wants to sell all of this land. We must get all the money we can from our families and buy it all up. Then we must file the claim for the mineral rights and sell the rights to some big oil company. We will make a lot of money." Angel said.

"But Angel, we still need water." Diego said.

Marcos, Diego and Angel hurried home to their families and collected every cent from every person they could find and hurried the very next day to the Pacifica State Administration Building in the city of Peace.

It was a long, hot, uncomfortable drive in their old truck and when they entered the main building they had to wait in line while other people were serviced.

Each of the three men carried two large bags of money with him and when their number was called, they labored to carry them to the counter.

"May I help you gentlemen?" She said.

"We wish to buy the land we have marked on this map, Ma'am." Angel said.

"Ah yes, the Vizcaino Desert. Let me find the price for that parcel. Here is the book." The woman laid out the price book and the four of them searched the pages for the correct parcel.

"The price is twenty cents per acre, how much do you want to buy." She said.

The three men hoisted the sacks onto the counter.

"We would like to buy this much, ma'am." Marcos said.

It took all afternoon to count the money and complete the necessary paperwork for the purchase of all the land between El Arco and San Ignacio stretching from the Pacific coast to the Gulf coast.

"You have fifty one dollars and thirty six cents left, now." She said.

"is there a charge to file a claim for mineral rights for this land, ma'am?" Angel asked.

"No sir, the mineral rights are included in the sale. Here look at this paragraph." She said.

"Then this money is your tip." Marcos said.

The three men laughed loudly and strode out the door as if they already had the millions of dollars they dreamed of.

Marcos, Diego and Angel made a few quiet contacts to the major oil companies for information about selling oil claims to their company. Soon there were men in black pinstripe suits knocking on their front doors.

The North American Oil Company was the first to visit the desert with the cash in hand. The borrowed water well drilling equipment was still in place just as they had left it that day.

"My company will give twenty dollars per acre for this land if we find oil where you say."

"Make it two hundred dollars and we will sell two hundred acres and guarantee the oil to be there. But we will not sell the land on the east side of Highway One." Marcos said.

The sale was completed and North American Oil trucked equipment in from the upper forty-eight for weeks until the new rig was set up and drilling resumed. Less than an hour after all the new equipment and derrick was erected at the spot where that old truck had been, the first well came in. Much to the delight of Marcos and his friends and several of the oil company executives who were there to watch the drilling begin.

Word spread quickly through the other oil company's grapevines and suddenly there was a rush to Pacifica to explore the discovery and try to get their piece of the action.

Marcos and his two associates had withheld a large chunk of the original purchase and now the price was two hundred dollars per acre for this land. The land was then broken up into one hundred acre plots.

It wasn't long before the three men were no longer land owners again. Each of the men deposited the sum of one million dollars in The First National

Bank of Monterrey, and each of their friends and relatives had large deposits in the same bank.

"Angel, do you think you will ever go back home?" Marcos asked.

"Marcos this is my home now. And we don't have to walk around in that stinking desert no more." Angel said.

They all laughed for weeks after that.

Coolie has been discussing the various powers of this unusual theta particle with some of his learned friends for many years. A doctor in a research lab in Ohio put one tiny theta particle in a tiny capsule and had the patient sniff it into his lungs.

The result was that each breath the patient drew caused the tiny capsule to move around the walls of the lung in the turbulence and the particle radiated the cancer cells until they were all dead. The patient was cured of a long standing case of lung cancer.

In typical research thinking, the question was asked, "If it will cure lung cancer, then why not the other cancers?" During preliminary tests, The researchers injected theta particles directly into cancerous areas, and the particle killed the growths in only hours. All that was left for the researchers to do was to calculate number of particles for each of the various types of tumors.

The New England Journal of Medicine ran an article in the June issue by Dr. Leonard Munsinger explaining the curative powers of the theta particles. The article detailed the Theta particle's ability to cure a person of any and all viruses known to man. Dr. Munsinger went on to say that these particles are available to the scientific community and should be made available to doctors and hospitals for medical uses.

The following month, in the July issue, the American Medical Association said in a letter to the editor that the opinions expressed in the article were not necessarily the opinions of the AMA.

This letter disagreed with Dr. Munsinger and said that more testing was necessary to come to such unbelievable conclusions. The AMA refused to authorize the use of this particle for any medical uses.

It wasn't long before people began to clamber for theta particles from doctors and hospitals all across the country to cure all kinds of maladies.

From the first day of his term, Mitchell has talked to every Senator and Congressman who will listen about the sins of the Indians and Hispanics and what to do about them. Slowly after his persistent pounding on the ears of his colleagues, he convinced some of the members that he was right.

Just before the Congressional break, the Congress tasked the Department of the Interior and their Division of Indian Affairs with the job of identifying members, assembling into groups and relocating all Indians on lands in the Northwest Territories and Greenland.

It was Monday after the break, that the men in Mitchell's office began the gloating.

"I never thought you could do it, Mitchell."

"I put my mind to it. How is the job in the islands going?" Mitchell said.

"Nearly all the whites are gone."

"Good! Now send in all your men with their cameras and completely remove everyone from my islands. Begin with Jamaica, then Puerto Rico, Columbus and last will be Cuba. With Congress out on vacation, no one will notice."

The shadow troops purified Jamaica in two weeks and set up residence in the Capital. All records were burnt and by the end of that week, it appeared that no one had ever lived on the island except for the existing buildings.

Donald McLeod was appointed Governor of Jamaica and his hand-picked associates brought in to rebuild the government. All land has been recorded in the name of Mitchell Cordel as the owner of record and during the following week, the cycle began anew on Puerto Rico.

Mitchell tasked a team of his troops to rename every inch of every island. All cities, towns, streets and other conspicuous points were renamed with English names.

Fred, Elia and their many friends and workers expanded the MacKenzie area to five domes. Tunnels were finally finished connecting all the domes and the three entrances from the nearby rocks.

It only took four months to complete the task of purifying the islands. Mitchell sent his people to claim all of the land for him and by the end of this little exercise he owned, on paper, all of the four islands of the Caribbean.

"Carlos, I mean Chuck, you are now in charge of selling all the land to businesses to build hotels, resorts, airports, shopping centers and anything else you can think of that will make us a lot of money." Mitchell said.

Just as Mitchell had predicted, big business bought everything in sight in the islands. Each of his men were allowed one parcel of real estate for their trouble. Mitchell of course, negotiated with the various buyers to build a personal mansion for him on each of the islands and furnish them with all the finest appointments which could be found.

Petroleum City was built at the inner most point of Scammon Lagoon off of Vizcaino Bay on the Pacific side of the peninsula of Pacifica. North American Oil hurried to build a refinery near the water to process the crude into fuel and service tankers, trains, trucks and a pipeline. The lagoon inside the bay was thought to be the best place for tankers to anchor while being filled with fuels from the refinery.

"The sites should be flat with no trees for the refinery and all the processing and loading operations. We will need bulldozers to prepare roads to town, and bring the rigging in."

"All the preparations have been made for the derricks and support equipment and make sure there isn't a tree in sight."

Business was booming here as well. Hotels, dorms for workers cafes and restaurants sprang up out of the ground nearly as fast as the oil from the wells. Employment rose steadily as workers prepared the sites for the new construction.

By the middle of November, the first hotel in the Caribbean Islands was opened for occupancy by the new owners. Resorts, hotels and all manner of new construction was continuing on all of the islands and Mitchell could not be happier.

Mitchell squirreled away all the money in various accounts in Swiss banking institutions.

"Do you know how much money we have in those accounts, Jolly?"

"Millions.

The money causes talk of the presidency from Jolly, Bobby and Carlos, and Mitchell is all smiles.

Chapter 13

Olympus

January 2035

Nineteen years ago, a blue planet was discovered by a probe from earth. Astronomers and engineers at NASA spent years researching every photo that was taken by the probe against star maps. These scientists finally feel certain that they have the location of this intriguing new life preserving planet.

"Anybody got an idea for a name for this new planet?"

"We could call it Hermes for the Greek god and protector of travelers."

"If we're going to use Greek gods, how about Aphrodite, goddess of love?"

"Or Eros?"

"Or Zeus?"

"You all may have a very good idea. Why not Olympus, the home of the gods? According to the Greek mythology, no one knew the location of Olympus because it was far away in the sky, and we sure had a hard time finding this."

"Good. Let's use that. We'll tell the press that we have named the new planet Olympus."

The trip to Kitty Hawk stirred quite a lot of interest among the dome lab gang. All of the information that Bruce wrote and recorded was analyzed and discussed by every member of the team. Bruce was able to remember the event clearly, which confused all of them.

"How is it that the subject loses his memory when we send them back from here, but does not when they return?" Fred asked.

This little bit of confusion persisted for some time until Casey interrupted the conversation.

"Coolie, when are you going to let me go back and see my Teresa?"

"I agree, let's send Casey to see what happened to his wife, maybe we can find out who did it and Casey can follow them back to the leader." Bruce said.

"Let's do it right away." Casey said.

"Alright then, let's set it up." Coolie said.

While the others completed their individual tasks and arranged and adjusted the equipment for this trip, Casey gathered the personal items he would need for this journey. This one was important and he didn't want to forget anything.

"Don't forget to put him there a few days before the actual event."

When all preparations had been made, checked and double checked, Casey assumed the position Bruce had taken previously.

FLASH!

It was a cool day with the sun shining as Casey found himself standing on a sidewalk at the corner of Musser and Carson Streets. He was dressed in civilian clothes, he didn't want to attract attention to himself. The uniform was left hanging in his closet in the dome. The memory module began to play into his ear, Fred's voice was speaking to him. He stood still until the voice stopped.

"Have a good time and we'll all see you soon, Case." Fred said.

According to plan he turned on the voice activated recorder and went to the nearest drug store.

"May I have a paper please?"

"Right there in the rack, sir." The clerk said.

The clerk was a tall brown haired teenager of barely eighteen.

"The Carson Chronicle, Carson City, Nevada, December 10, 2031."

"That's the one." He said.

"Do you have the correct time, my watch seems to have stopped."

"Sure, it's three thirty seven."

Casey set his watch and hurried across the street to the Capital Building and up the stairs to Teresa's office. He had four days to be with her before she would be sent across to the other side and he wanted to spend every moment with her that he could.

He entered her office quietly and stood in front of her desk. She was writing notes on a pad and looking at the computer screen.

"I'll be right with you sir." She said.

"Quite alright, ma'am, I have the rest of my life to wait for you."

She looked up with a start as she heard that very familiar voice.

"Casey!"

She jumped up like she had springs in her feet, just like she always did when Casey was with her. She grabbed him and kissed him there in the office with everyone watching.

"Casey! Casey! Casey!" Teresa screamed.

"I think she likes him." One of the others said and the rest of them laughed.

"Teresa, it's almost four o'clock. Why don't you and your husband go on home." The supervisor said.

Teresa grabbed her coat and ran for the door, dragging Casey behind her. He had to run to keep up, but he didn't mind one bit. He was with the love of his life, maybe for the last time of his life.

"We don't have to get the boys from the baby-sitter until five o'clock. Want to see my house?" She said.

He drove her four wheel drive van and she hugged him all the way to the house on Paloverde Street.

It was five fifteen when Teresa broke the silence.

"Why don't you get the boys and I'll start dinner?" She said.

"I don't know where they are, honey." He said.

"You know, the second house from the corner of Fifth and Valley, Mrs. Romero."

Casey didn't know, but he could find her. He drove to the drug store and looked in the phone book for Mrs. Romero close to the corner where Tease told him. Ten minutes later he was hugging his two boys and they were screaming "Daddy". The four of them had dinner and played until bedtime when Teresa put them down. Casey was exhausted from the excitement of the boys and his wonderful wife.

"You wear me out, my love." He said.

"How long are you home for this time?"

"Four days."

"You have been working too hard on this Mexico thing, honey. You better take your naps during the day, because you're going to be a lot more worn out by then."

She was right.

During the day, Casey walked around town and tried to be as inconspicuous as he could. He was looking for the men with Spector who were marauding the Nevada countryside. On the morning of the fourth day he knew he must stay close to the house but not in the line of fire.

He had flown into the Municipal Airport at ten a.m. that day and drove straight home. At nine thirty, he hid himself next to the house across the street with his Infrared camera and waited. It was only a few minutes before two men, one carrying a large case and the other carrying a pouch with "Film" written on it, walked down the street.

Teresa was sitting on the swing with the boys as the men approached. The men spoke to her and as she answered, the one carrying the box turned it around and the flash of Spector lit up the house. Casey took his photos, put the camera back into his pocket and followed them down the street.

"No guts, no glory." Thought Casey.

"Hey guys!" He yelled.

The two men stopped and turned around as Casey ran up to them.

"You talkin' to us?"

"Yeah. Mitchell just called me and wanted you to call him. I've been looking all over town for you."

"Come on, we better get to a phone. You know how he is." The one carrying the "Film" bag said.

"I was right!" Casey said as he threw the AR switch in his pocket.

Casey was not the happiest guy in the world when he returned to the lab in the dome. No one had to start the conversation, he was seething inside.

"It was Mitchell! I told you it was! I'll kill him! I'll beat him to death, then I'll kill him!"

Casey's face was red and he was waving his arms and he started to beat on the desk as soon as he was close enough to it.

"Settle down and tell us everything that happened. Bruce, get the recorder and have it transcribed." Coolie said.

Casey told them every detail he could think of and cursed Mitchell between every sentence.

While Casey was away in Carson City, Roger Pond sent a message to Bruce at the dome lab that he wanted to see Casey in his office at NASA in Houston as soon as he returned from his junket.

"You want me to fly to this new planet Olympus? What kind of craft could possibly make a trip like that? It would take decades to return and I'm not willing to give up my hunt for Teresa for a trip like this." Casey said.

"NASA let a contract back in the twenties for a space plane to fly to this new planet and there are two of these planes in a hangar at Nellis Air Force Base in Nevada waiting for this specific purpose." Roger said.

"It'll still take too long for the trip." Casey said.

"Not with the combination of the two power sources we have at our disposal." Roger said.

"I already know about Roamer, but that will only make the plane go at the speed of light."

"By combining Spector into the equation, we will be able to move in time as well." Roger said.

"OK, so even if all this baloney is true, how long will the trip take? From the time the plane leaves earth until it returns?" Casey asked.

"We think about two or three months one way, but we need an experienced pilot, you." Roger said.

"Pilot? I can't fly a plane for two months straight! You need a qualified crew! Talk to me when you have a crew and have made a couple of test flights to someplace like Saturn or Pluto or farther."

"That has all been accomplished. Did you think we have been sitting on our hands for all these years?" Roger said.

"Let's see the results and I want to talk to the crew and the engineers." Casey said.

"Fred Goss is implementing the integration of Spector into the plane's systems as we speak."

"I thought Fred was working with us." Casey said.

"He was. Yes he is. Off and on he would come when I screamed for help."

"OK, I'll contact Fred for his take on the interface between systems of the spacecraft, the computer, the craft and the pilot. If he gives it a go then I'll try one flight. But the hunt for Teresa, and how to save her, is still my number one priority." Casey said.

Back at the dome lab Casey pulled Fred aside for some very special discussion.

"Fred, what's the story on the space plane out there at Nellis and does it work?"

"Casey, I think I have all the bugs worked out of the systems, but I need to complete the installation of the autopilot. Then we'll do one more shakedown flight and it should be ready to go." Fred said.

That Friday, Fred and Casey flew to Nellis to study for two months with the astronomers and engineers who were working on this project. Chuck Kinkaid met them at the airport when the plane landed. Fred and Chuck took Casey through every step and every system as a training exercise.

After much consideration and thought, Casey decided to fly one trip to Olympus. With Roamer, there was no need for a booster rocket, the plane will taxi and take off from any airport like a large plane and fly to one hundred thousand feet. The whole trip should take about two months from the eleven million mile point above the Earth to Olympus acquisition.

"Hey Case, phone." Chuck said.

"Casey, the engineers report to me that the space plane is ready to go. We'll make our first flight to the new planet on the tenth of June from Kennedy. Will you be able to go on this one?" Roger said.

"Yeah, Roger. Fred gave me a full briefing on the craft. I think I can make the trip."

"Great! See you in Florida."

"Computer, recognize Casey MacKenzie." Casey said.

A young familiar sounding female voice answered.

"Good morning, Commander. How may I help you?"

"Recognize crew members Brad Hart, Co-pilot, George Stinson, Engineering Officer, Peter Tower, Navigation Officer and Carl Bullock, Communications Officer." Casey said.

Each of the crew members spoke to the computer after Casey said their name.

"Crew recognized. Standing by."

"All systems on." Casey said.

"Systems on."

"Secure all openings and prepare for flight."

"Ready."

"Begin takeoff roll." The huge plane began to move forward down the runway.

"Increase power and come to one hundred thousand feet, straight and level." The plane lifted off the runway and flew smoothly and easily to a hundred thousand feet where it leveled off.

"Show our present position and heading on main screen."

The main screen lit with a small plane shaped icon on a dotted line around a representation of the Earth.

"Engage Roamer and proceed to point A. Execute."

The computer engaged Roamer for one minute and the craft traveled to the predetermined point in space, eleven million miles above the earth.

"Show course, speed and time duration of journey to Olympus."

The main screen presentation changed to the plane icon on a dotted line from one globe to another.

"Computer."

"Yes sir."

"Energize Spector and set time to 1933 and engage Auto Return for return along same course."

"Yes sir, time set, Auto Return set, engaging memory module to play into speaker."

"Lay in preset course to Olympus."

"Course laid in."

"Execute." Casey said.

"Good evening. This is World News Tonight for June 10th, 2035. A trans-space transport plane left for Olympus from Kennedy Space Center, Florida. This giant space plane is transporting one thousand people to the newly discovered planet named Olympus to settle and build a new civilization."

"These people have all volunteered for this exciting and dangerous life. After four hours for boarding and unloading each way, the trip is thought to take about two months to Olympus."

"Originally NASA has planned three trips for volunteers for the colonization of this new world. This adventure could be quite a hardship for all concerned. These people must build or grow everything to make a new life for themselves."

Casey was exhausted from the trip to Olympus and back, but as soon as his foot touched solid ground he was thinking of only one thing, Teresa. The whole gang met him at Nellis when he landed and all of them had questions about everything he could think of.

"Wait! I'll brief you on everything that happened and you may have the recorders, but before any of that happens, I made a deal with Roger before this trip and I want to know if that deal is still good."

"Yes. It is." Roger said.

"Good, let's get to work. It's October tenth, and I only have a month to spend with you. I have an important appointment." Casey said.

It was easier for Casey to provide a briefing with everyone in the room and explain the trip from beginning to end than to try to answer questions helter-skelter the way they usually came.

"Alright, is everyone ready? Let me begin with the takeoff. It was a very uneventful takeoff, the crew and I fit well together. Roamer and Spector did the assigned tasks with speed and accuracy.

"I was very surprised that all this super-technical fru-fru worked as it was designed. One little concern, we used a lot of fuel during the beginning and end of the trip, but almost none during the part of the trip between point A and acquisition. This might be something you should examine."

"With computer control, the journey was much easier. Once we had Roamer, Spector and Autopilot on and functioning, the crew could stand down from alert and only one man stand watch on the flight deck."

"This new world, Olympus, is covered with three large continents stretching from one pole to the other and divided by three large oceans. The continents are connected at the poles, which are, just like ours, covered with white snow and ice."

"The beautiful blue of the oceans, seas, lakes and rivers are much like earth, but before man ruined everything here. There are mountains, some snow capped, and green meadows on every continent. We flew several times around the world searching for a place to land that huge plane. Everyone took many photos and the computer recorded it all on video."

"During the trip, many friendships were consciously made between the passengers, people were looking for mates and friends to build a life together. The crew made some friends as well, but for much different reasons. The passengers elected ten Governors to begin organizing and regulating the start of their new civilization. I have a list of their names."

"Once we saw the blue globe in the distance, the passengers seemed to take on a euphoria, and everyone was ecstatic through the acquisition procedure and even until landing was completed."

"Once we had landed, we had to unload one thousand passengers, their baggage pods, the equipment pods, ten motorized equipment carriers and one Commutercopter that would be used for reconnaissance."

"During landing, we found that the best procedure was this. Spector off upon acquisition of the planet, Roamer off at eleven million miles out, assume an orbital posture, move to sub orbital position, Earth engines on, all flaps down, land on any flat surface."

"There did not appear to be human life on the planet. We saw plants and animals, but no human or other such species that we could see from the plane." Casey said.

"How'd you like the computer, Case?" Chuck asked.

"Worked great, but I knew that voice, I just couldn't put my finger on it."

"We synthesized Yvonne's voice."

After Mitchell and his closest associates, Bobby, Jolly and Chuck picked the land they wanted to retain for themselves, the business of tearing down shacks and towing away junk cars and trucks before hotels could be built began the complete renovation of the islands.

San Juan, the Capital of Puerto Rico, was one of the first cities to undergo the renaming process. It became Johnstown on the island of Richland.

Since this island became the beginning of the "Caribbean Project" as Mitchell called it, Caribbean Real Estate, owned by Mitchell, opened its first office there. Mitchell hired managers and real estate agents for all the CRE offices. Of course, CRE enjoyed an exclusive listing of all land on all four of the islands. Something of a monopoly.

Several new resort and hotel operators have built on each of the four islands. Autumn Leaves Resorts, a sprawling resort covering many acres around the bay on the western shore of Columbus is the biggest and best known of the resorts any where in the Caribbean. Canary Isle Resorts is a much smaller, but no less successful resort. Its cottage type living and easy slow style has captured the eye of many tourists.

Hotels are sprouting up around the islands as well. Hilliard House Hotel, a huge concrete, stone and marble luxury hotel built only in the best places on the islands cater to the richest of the tourist trade. On the other side of the coin, Country Inns is a much smaller more personal and homey hotel. It is cheaper, serves home cooking, is always full, and there is one in every town on each island.

"As soon as hotels are built, bring people in to work in the hotels. Give them houses. Tell them to just pick the house they want and move in. Tell them to take a car or truck that might be sitting around. The can live there free for as long as they will work for us and populate the islands." Mitchell said.

Small business men were invited from the mainland with the lure of free stores, all they had to do was pay taxes. They came in large numbers. Money is pouring in to Mitchell and his associates.

On November 10th, Casey was in the lab with all his friends making preparations for a very special journey. He would be the first to go across to wherever Teresa and all the others were sent. Casey has made very extensive and careful preparations for this unbelievable passage.

Coolie, Bruce and Chuck had made a pre-flight checklist for time trips and were checking off each item one by one just as a pilot would do before take-off.

"Is everyone ready?" Casey, please stand on your mark. I don't want any screw ups on this one. We need him back here next year for another trip to Olympus." Roger said.

FLASH!

Casey found himself standing on the same corner where he had stood just a few months ago, but there were many noticeable differences. The sky was a bright blue and the air was clean and crisp and smelled good. The module played into his ear as Roger read the pre-packaged script to him. Casey walked to the drugstore and bought a paper from a different clerk, she was a short dark-haired girl of about twenty.

"The Carson Chronicle, Carson City, Nevada, November 10 2035."

The sun was shining, the sky was blue and there was that same crisp cool smell in the air that he remembered from times past. Casey reset his watch and walked across the street to the Capital building and up the stairs to Teresa's office.

The Capital Building was strangely empty, the receptionist with whom he had talked so many times was not at the Information Desk. Teresa was sitting at her desk as Casey entered the office, but there were only three others there with her.

"Casey! Honey!" She said.

She jumped up as she always did and grabbed him and hugged and kissed him.

"I hope you can stay a while. I've missed you so much." She said.

"The plan is for me to stay until February, maybe longer."

Maria, it's Friday and I don't have anything to do, I'm going to take off for the rest of the day." Tease said.

"OK Teresa, see you Monday." She said.

During the next several days Casey made some very interesting discoveries. Teresa is still living in the same house on Paloverde street with the two boys, and she has sent the house payment in every month but it always came back "undeliverable" about three weeks later.

She went to the mortgage company once with her payment, but there was no one there and the doors were locked. That day, she voided the checks and put the cash payments in the freezer every month.

"How long have you been doing this?" He asked.

"Ever since you were here the last time." She said.

He retrieved the two sacks from the freezer in the basement and they counted the money.

"Thirty eight thousand eight hundred dollars." He said. "You just keep putting it away until I tell you different. It's a great idea, and don't tell anyone."

"Do you know that this house is a hundred years old this year and we have been in it for thirteen years now?"

As always the boys tire him out, but now both are four years older than the last time he saw them, which was only a few months ago. It's hard for Casey to think about such problems, he just let it go until they can find a way to resolve it all. Sean is twelve and becoming a fine young man, Billy is seven and still a rambunctious kid. Casey has his hands full with these two.

It was one of the best weekends he had enjoyed for many years, except the one most recently spent with Teresa. The four of them talked and played around the house, with the football and the baseball. Casey ran and chased all three of them all day long until he was lying on the front lawn and couldn't move.

"Come on dad. I'm ready." Billy said.

"Ohhh."

"What's the matter, Case. Did I get to you?" She asked.

"Ohhh."

Teresa climbed on top of him and the boys on her and they all bounced on Casey and laughed.

"Ohhh."

Teresa asked Casey if he would go with her to shop for Thanksgiving dinner. Of course Casey said he would, he is committed to be with her for every waking, and sleeping, hour of every day. There isn't much in the grocery stores, but it's getting better all the time.

They have to shop a little here and a little there to get the things they need for the dinner. Finally they got it all and returned home with their valuable purchases. There hasn't been turkey in the stores for four years, but they bought four big roasting chickens, potatoes, green beans, and sweet potatoes for pies.

It was a good day for all of them. Casey and they boys were rough housing around the back yard until Teresa would call him for some help with dinner. They would all stop and help mom and run out to the back yard and begin again. Casey made sure to hug and kiss Tease every time he was close to her. This made Teresa feel good and the boys knew that mom and dad were still there for them.

It took all day to get the dinner ready, but Teresa called them in to get cleaned up at two o'clock. The dinner looked and smelled wonderful. The four chickens were carefully cut into pieces with mashed potatoes and gravy, green beans and hot biscuits. The sweet potato pies were kept warm in the oven.

"Before we start to eat, I would like to say a Thanksgiving Prayer." She took the two boys hands in hers and they all made a ring with their hands.

"Thank you Lord for bringing our beloved husband and father back home to us for this very special day in our lives. Please protect him in all that he does, so that he may be with us for a long time." She said.

"Wait. I have a prayer too. Thank you Lord for showing me these things and please show me the way to resolve all these problems." He said.

It was comfortable for Casey to be home with Tease and the boys during the Holidays, but everything was so strange. For example, even though there was television, some of the channels he had watched before were not on the air, and some only transmitted during the day.

Thanksgiving Day has always been a tradition for professional and college football games to be played. Casey noticed that if there was a football game shown on the television, that the only players to be seen on the field and sidelines were black and Hispanic.

Now that he knew that Mitchell was behind the removal of all these people he could understand who was the target of his anger, black and Hispanic people. But what could Casey do?

Casey has such a hunger for Teresa and the boys that even in his lax moments, he thinks of new ways to entertain and interest them with fun and enjoyment. They drove over to the lake with a picnic basket and took a boat out on the water to fish for a couple of hours. There were several bites but most of them were from marauding mosquitoes and other vermin flying around, but not one fish was caught.

There were a few Christmas parties at work and three with friends, but some of Teresa's friends didn't know Casey.

"Who is that man you're with tonight, Teresa? You're always alone at these functions. I have never met him or saw him around here before." One woman asked.

"Don't you know my husband, Casey?"

It hurt him when the woman asked the question and he sat down with a drink for a long time.

Casey took every opportunity to hold, hug and kiss Teresa, and dancing was a very good excuse. They danced at every party. They danced when there wasn't music. They danced on the street. They danced in the living room. Best of all Casey told Teresa that he loved her during every dance.

"Do you remember when I was home last, a guy with a camera? He asked.

"I saw two men with a camera stop at the gate and take our picture, after the flashbulb went off they weren't there anymore."

He showed a photo of them to her that he took on the sidewalk that day.

"Yes, that's them."

New Years Eve parties are always fun to attend and after Teresa arranged with the lady down the street to watch the boys, she and Casey were off for a long night of merriment and dancing.

There weren't many parties around town, but Teresa and Casey did go to the ones they could find and drank a toast here and there and danced and had a lot of fun. At the appointed time, they were with well wishers to ring in the New Year 2036.

They all tried to watch the football games on New Years Day, but the reception still isn't what it should be.

One of the very best parts of the New Year was when the family celebrated two birthdays together on the same day.

"Happy birthday, my love. May you have many more, and may I be blessed with attending every one of them." He said.

"Happy birthday to you too Casey." She said.

Governor Martin Gonzalez was standing in the hallway when Casey came out of Teresa's office.

"Good afternoon Casey. Teresa tells me that you have made another grade since I saw you last. I have something important to discuss with you, will you walk with me?"

They walked along the hallway as Martin spoke.

"Senator Wilson is missing and feared dead, would you consider the job? If you will take it, I can appoint you to fill the balance of his term. Re-election would be up to you at the end of the term." Martin said.

"I'll talk to my wife. Now I have a question for you. Do you remember two guys with a big bulky camera?"

"Yes. There were two men who did group photos all around town. There were ads in the paper and on TV about free photos of your business or organization." He said.

"Did it seem strange to you that these guys disappeared right after the photos were taken?" Casey asked.

"Yes, they took our picture and after the flashbulb went off they disappeared. But we didn't think anything of it at the time."

"Did they do anything else that you thought was strange?"

"Come to think of it, you're right. They selected some of the people out of the photos and had them stand aside. You know, those people aren't to be found now. The receptionist was one of them. Do you suppose these people were harmed by them, Casey?"

"Governor, I can tell you with authority that those people are safe, and if I have anything to do about it, you will see them soon." Casey said.

Chapter 14

Flights Of Fancy

March 2036

"I talked with Teresa and Governor Martin Gonzalez and showed the pictures of the two men who I saw flash her with the Spector. She remembered the two guys and so did the Governor. Martin told me that they serviced most of the corporate structure of the city with photos of their employees, but what was most amazing about what the Governor told me was that some of the people were selected out of the photos of the Capital Building personnel prior to the photos.

"I contacted one of the selected people who had taken pictures with a real camera and here they are." Casey said.

Casey handed the pictures to Bruce and Chuck who passed them around to the others.

"All of these people are white, brown haired or blonde and Anglo Saxon or other nationality similar to that. I'll bet they think that they are killing off all the black, Indian and Mexican people when they take their pictures."

"I've got to go to Carson City to see the Governor and the house on Paloverde street." Casey said.

The house is sitting empty, just as he had hoped, but Casey has always carried a key with him. He used the key and let himself into his little house. All the furniture was still there and dishes and silverware are in the cabinets.

As he walked around he took note of every item in the house and compared it with the house he had seen only weeks ago on the other side. It was identical with some small exceptions.

Now it is time to really do some investigating. Casey headed down to the basement and straight to the freezer. He opened the freezer and looked for the bags that Teresa has been using for the house payment. Sure enough, the bags were there. That means that Teresa is there too. But where? He can't see her.

Casey has a lot of work to do to make sense of the clues he has. The next stop has to be the Capital Building and the Governor's Office. The name on the door said James Fairhope, Governor.

"Good afternoon sir, my name is John Jones and I wanted to talk to you for a few minutes." Casey said.

Casey has been carrying that unusual medal they removed from the man's neck in the woods outside the dome ever since he saw it. He took it out of his pocket and wound it around his fingers as he extended his hand to shake the Governor's hand.

"I see you and I have some of the same friends, Mr. Jones. How can I help you?" Governor Fairhope said.

"So that's what this is all about." He said to himself.

Flying back and forth from Nellis Air Base and Carson City and the dome has become drudgery for

Casey, but he is learning with each trip. Back at the dome, Chuck came to Casey with a wild and crazy idea. They want to put Theta particles on him and study him at various steps to see what it does to him.

"Sure, give me some of that Theta, I'm feelin' my rage about now." He said.

The experiments went well for several weeks, with the dosage increasing by twenty parts per million each week. Casey showed no signs of rage or any other unusual traits during the whole course of the testing. During this time, he explained everything he had learned up till now and asked them for ideas.

"We have increased the dosage in your body to two hundred PPM Casey, but you haven't shown the first bit of rage." Chuck said.

"Not any more than normal, that is." Bruce said.

"Look guys, it's been fun, but I have a flight to make and a thousand people are depending on me. I'll check in as soon as I get that big plane back."

"Before you go, maybe you could think about this, if the house payment is there, and from that then Teresa is there, maybe there is a way you could communicate with her if you were there too." Fred said.

"Bruce, you know Tease. Could you go live in the house while I'm gone and maybe you'll get some kind of inspiration? Please?" Casey practically begged Bruce.

NASA has scheduled six regular flights for the spaceplanes to Olympus on a six month basis. Casey will take the next flight this week. The combination of Roamer and Spector and the spaceplane's on board computer made the trips not only possible, but even enjoyable for all concerned. If it wasn't for these monumental inventions, the trips to Olympus would be completely impossible.

Casey's second flight to Olympus with his crew mates was as enjoyable as the first flight. It was becoming a routine almost like flying around the world in a commercial plane and they were glad of it.

During such a long flight, the crew has many opportunities to interact with the passengers. One item which was brought up by several passengers was that they wanted to be able to land on a different part of the new world away from the others in order that these new immigrants could start their own way of life.

Once the spaceplane was in sub orbital position, the passengers were staring out the windows hoping for a glimpse of their choice of their new home. Suddenly the cry was heard, "There it is!" Several passengers had seen the same place at the same time and one of them ran forward to the flight deck to inform the crew of the place to land.

The crew and the passengers searched for a flat and level place to put the huge plane down and finally someone spotted a suitable place.

This new world has no people and no buildings, only animals and flora, and those could be quite strange. There is, however, lots of blue water, blue sky and food hanging on trees and plants. Everyone is excited to disembark and begin exploring the new countryside.

The passenger list from each trip includes doctors, educators, builders, architects, tradesmen, farmers and many other categories of educated and uneducated people.

No matter the level of education, the excitement of setting foot on a far off world from Earth is exhilarating for all concerned. In this diverse mix of people there is always a few who have the vision to see what might be, what could be.

One of the passengers asked him. "You're a pilot and a logical man, Casey. What do you see as the first thing we should do on this new world?"

"Of course, food and shelter come to mind first, but you're not talking about that. It would be a big help if there were an airport for this spaceplane to land safely. That would make future flights more likely." He said.

The flight back with a completely empty plane was also somewhat exciting for the crew. They had just seeded a new world with humans who will breed a new race of people and populate that whole world. These new inhabitants must build houses and begin farming and fending for themselves to start a new civilization.

People have been flocking to the islands to live and work in the sunny paradise of the Caribbean. More than half of the residents of the islands work for Mitchell and his businesses and enjoy living rent free. All of the other residents work for one of the many resorts or are small businessmen invited to the islands by the generous gifts advertised in the press.

The largest and most beautiful bay and the one place where all the most exclusive resorts headed for was the Bay of Gonave on the western coast of Columbus. The name of the bay will be changed to another fine English name as soon as Mitchell thinks of one.

Although Autumn Leaves Resorts built a sprawling resort covering many acres around the bay on the western shore of Columbus, other resorts soon began to build in the same area.

It won't be long before resorts ring the Bay of Georgia and the tiny Isle of Georgia in the center of the bay.

From the town of Jeremy to Princeport to Saint Mark and on to the tiny island of Tortuga, land has been sold to resort and hotel chains from all around the world.

"Mitchell, we have tallied the latest sales and deposited all receipts to the Swiss Account, it now stands at just over fifty million."

"Good, we seem to all be working together." He said smugly.

Ken and Chuck have been working in the lab in Houston all this time and attending the weekly meetings by vidphone. Every now and then one of them drops a bomb in the meeting.

"We believe that we know why the particles fall off a purified person. The particles don't belong on the other side, because the comet was never there."

"How do you know this?" Ken said.

"We don't know it, but it's the only theory that makes sense."

"Why wasn't it there?"

"We don't know that either, but it wasn't." He said.

Casey went directly to the house from the landing strip at Nellis. Bruce answered the door.

"Please tell me that you have something."

"A little, I think, but you'll have to see it for yourself." Bruce said.

There was a note laying on the table. Casey picked it up and read it.

"What's so special about this, it's Teresa's writing, but there would be things like this in the house."

"It appeared last night, in answer to a note I left on the table here."

Bruce pointed to the place on the dining room table that he had left the note.

"Do you know what this means?" Casey said.

Casey sat down and stared at the note.

"I need more proof. Both of our birthdays are coming up this month. I'm going to get her a birthday present and leave it on the table with a little note for her. Do you know how old I am? I'm too old for this." Casey said.

"Yes, the same age as I am." Bruce said.

Casey hurried to the shopping mall and bought a beautiful crystal vase and filled it with roses from the florist shop and poured his heart out with love for Teresa in a birthday card.

The gift was placed on the dining room table and Bruce and he waited and watched the vase and its contents.

Casey looked at his watch. It was five o'clock.

"She will be picking up the boys at the sitter in the next few minutes and they should be walking in that door in about ten minutes."

Bruce and Casey sat at the table and stared at the vase.

Suddenly the vase disappeared.

"There!" Bruce screamed.

The card was still on the table and as Casey stood up it disappeared as well.

"I declare now to you that I am going to stop Mitchell no matter what I have to do. This is only one life that he has ruined. There must be hundreds, maybe thousands, more who are affected too. This will be my life's work! Damn him!" Casey was seething.

"I have a lot of work to do. You must contact Coolie and the rest of them and explain what we have found here. I don't know what we can do with it yet, but I think the answer is right here at the tips of our fingers." Casey told Bruce.

Casey hurried out to find a coin shop in the mall.

"Yes I have all sorts of gold coins. How many would you like, sir?" He said.

"I would like to but five thousand dollars worth of gold coins. When can you deliver them?"

"I have that much in my safe now, sir."

"Good, I'll be right back with the money."

Casey hurried back to the house and counted out five thousand dollars from the freezer. The clerk spread the coins out on the glass of the display case.

"Would you happen to have a small box, maybe metal, plastic or wood, that these would fit into? I don't want to carry this around in a little plastic bag."

Casey hurried back to the house and carefully placed the box in the very bottom back corner of the freezer. Casey was a very conservative man when it came to anything about Teresa and knowing what Mitchell has already accomplished, the money in the freezer could be worthless by tomorrow, but gold will never go out of style.

While Bruce was traveling back to the dome, Casey replaced every last piece of paper money with gold coins and hid them in the same place as before.

Casey felt better now that he knew Teresa was living there in the house with him. He had been busy with the flights and running around the country. This kind of thing tires a man out. Now that Bruce was gone and he was in the house alone, with Teresa, he could finally rest for a while.

Casey fell asleep on the couch. It was a good quiet sleep with no one to disturb him.

He was walking into the Capital building with Martin and two other men and down the hall to the Senate Chamber. He walked up to the front of the room with Martin and they all sat in the front row while Martin stepped to the podium and began to speak to the people gathered in the great room.

Suddenly the scene changed to Teresa sitting on his lap with the boys playing in the living room and dinner was being served at the dining room table. How could that be? Teresa was there on his lap.

He woke up with a start and looked around. The house was still as empty as it was before, but he had a funny feeling that the dream living room was not in this house. What a strange feeling, it was so real.

He laid back down to complete his nap.

During the time that Bruce was gone to the dome, Casey searched through the house for answers. He decided to can give a present to Teresa and the boys. Valentine's Day was just next week and it was a good excuse. He left the Valentines for the boys on the table, a special one on the bed for Teresa. As before when they came home after work and school, they found them and they disappeared.

Now that he knows they are there in the house, it's time try something really hard. He moved around the house slowly trying to be where Teresa would be if they were there together. For an instant he thought he saw, in his mind, her doing laundry in the basement. He ran down the stairs to be with her.

It was as if he could see her but not speak to her. He reached out for her and she turned slightly and spoke to him. He couldn't hear her and suddenly he couldn't see her either.

He stood there in the basement alone looking at the washer which was not running, wondering what was happening to him. He knew his presence was felt, but how could he contact her?

The next day he bought her a card and after inscribing a nice note on it, put it on the table and kept his hand on it. He had placed himself at the table with a clear view of the clock on the wall. It seemed like a long wait for five o'clock, and even longer for five fifteen, sixteen, twenty, thirty. Where is she?

When she came into the room, she saw the card and put her hand on it and he felt her hand on his. It's her! For an instant, he saw a cloudy figure of Teresa holding his hand, but as soon as she saw him it scared her and she moved her hand and the vision was gone.

It seemed that every time Casey found some kind of special information or something interesting happened, he had to go away. The next flight of the spaceplane to Olympus was due in less than a week and he was required to be there.

Bruce brought Chuck and Fred back to the house to do as Fred said, "a seance with the unseen living."

"We'll watch the house for you and we will work very hard to find the way to Teresa. I promise." Chuck said.

The flight to Olympus was uneventful and at some times even boring for Casey. During the long flight he would daydream about the woman he loved so much and then it happened. The visions he had in the house were, he thought, due to the nearness of Teresa and the house and their love a bond connecting them. But this.

The vision started out as if he were watching a movie. He saw Teresa and the boys, Martin and some other friends waving to him at the airport as he boarded the airplane. Not the spaceplane, just a commercial airplane. He talked with the stewardesses and the passengers and while he was retrieving his baggage, a man approached him and led him away to a waiting car.

The scene changed to the inside of an office and as he turned toward the door, he noted outside the window a distinctive structure which he recognized. But that building is in Washington DC and he had never been there. What was he seeing?

The scene changed several times showing men dressed in suits talking to him and shaking his hand. It was like a silent movie without the subtitles. Very disconcerting.

During the trip to and from Olympus the dreams, or visions, continued and even intensified. He saw Teresa and the boys many times, always in a different setting and under different circumstances.

Chuck was there when he parked the big plane and disembarked with the crew. They drove to Carson City and directly to the house. The whole gang was at the house when Chuck and Casey walked in from the airport. Coolie introduced Dr. Cameron Robbins, a psychologist, to the group.

"What is this, you think I'm crazy?" Casey said.

"No, not at all. A psychologist studies things affecting the mind, the science of human behavior. A psychiatrist is someone who does treatment of

disorders of the mind. No one thinks you're crazy."
Coolie said.

"Casey, I'm a late comer into this group, so would
you please explain what you have been experienc-
ing." The doctor said.

"I see things regularly as if I were there and was
seeing it through my own eyes, people speak to me
and call me by name in these visions."

"One thing, we know why you are having these
so-called visions. You remember that they put Theta
particles on you last year? Dr. Kuhlmann and I believe these particles are allowing you to see into the
other timeline. That would be why things appear
cloudy." Dr. Robbins said.

"That's ridiculous!"

"No. Listen. You remember that Governor Martin Gonzalez talked to you about filling the vacant
seat of the missing Senator named Clifford Wilson?"
Bruce said.

"Yes."

"Clifford Wilson is the Senator from Nevada right
now. On this side. Martin is on the other side with
Teresa. Wilson is missing on that side, because he's
here. Maybe you're filling his seat now, there." Bruce
said.

"I've got something for you. One of Teresa's most
recent notes says that Casey is in Washington DC."
Chuck said.

"I've had the same kind of feelings too, but I've
never been to DC." Casey said.

"We think that your alter ego remained with Teresa when you returned here. We think you accepted

the appointment that Martin offered." Dr. Robbins said.

"That means that I can go back to her." He said.

"No. There would be two of you there. We must find a way to correct a fault that happened. But we don't know how to correct it." Chuck said.

"Well we better find it soon. I have flown five trips to the mystery planet, and I'm going to fly one more flight and I'm finished with that. I want my wife back and I will do anything to get her." He said.

The house was empty again and Casey was alone in it. January comes around much too often, especially when your birthday is in January. He spent his and Teresa's birthday in the house alone.

"I'm thirty eight years old and married with two kids and here I sit in a vacant house celebrating by birthday."

Casey has been drinking for two weeks straight. It's not getting any better. He'll be alright soon, he has one more flight that he committed to Roger to fly. But that's next month, have another drink.

Casey has been writing notes and buying presents for Teresa and the boys, and Teresa has written back to him, but it hasn't helped. He can't see her. He can't hold her.

Casey is packing for the last of his six flights across the cosmos and suddenly he had an inspiration. He sat at the dining room table and wrote a note to Teresa.

"I have an important voyage to fly. I leave this item with you. Do everything you can to ferret out and eliminate all who worship it. Show it to Martin and anyone whom you can trust. These are the ones who have destroyed our country and are keeping us apart. I will be with you as soon as I can. Love, Case."

He placed the note on the table and the medal on top of it and walked out the door.

The trip felt better to Casey, knowing that it was the last for him. There were other pilots and another plane in the hangar back on the base in Nevada. It was time that he moved on to more important things.

The big plane landed and taxied to the assigned point for the crew to turn it over to the maintenance squadron. Casey was relieved when Bruce and Chuck met him at the Operations Building.

"Anything new?" Chuck asked.

"Not much. Let's go home."

The phone was ringing as they entered the house on Paloverde Street.

"Hello." Chuck picked it up.

"When?"

"What about the little one."

"OK. Thanks."

"What's up?" Bruce asked.

"The crew from the Maintenance Squadron were putting the plane into the hangar for the post-flight maintenance when a forklift ran into the side of the plane and it exploded. The hangar and both planes were destroyed. Six people killed." Chuck said.

Chapter 15
Cordel's Reign

July 2038

"What little one?" Casey asked.

"The little spaceplane prototype." Chuck said.

"What about it?"

"It wasn't damaged. It's in another hangar."

As Bruce and Chuck were talking, Casey looked for the medal and the note he left on the table. They were gone.

Pollution and ecology have been good points for election and reelection political rhetoric for decades. The earth's ecology was worse than ever and seemed a far better platform than any other. Many politicians used it for their own campaign. For years now, the sky has been a strange yellow brown color from the air pollution because the airborne theta particles make a strange light from the sun.

"Ya know, Case, you should run for that Senate seat you talked about." Bruce said.

"I don't know, I don't think I could win."

"We'll all help. Besides if you win you would be able to be closer to Mitchell, and maybe find a way to stop him." Chuck said.

"You're right. You convinced me. Let's do it."

Bruce and Chuck agreed to be Casey's campaign managers for the duration. Casey needs two managers in order to keep in contact with the work in the lab.

The election process is a long and difficult one. It is time consuming and energy taxing for the individual and all of the members of his campaign organization including volunteers. The year of 2039 was taken up with the election campaigns of Governors, Senators, Congressmen and a President. It seemed as if everyone in both houses of Congress threw their hat into the ring for President.

For some reason, this particular election year was deemed high profile by the television networks all across the country. There was television coverage of primaries, candidates stumping their local districts and every other part and parcel of the campaign year.

The New Hampshire primary was overloaded with more than a dozen hopefuls in each of the two parties. Mitchell was one of the six in his party who survived it and moved on to the next step.

Mitchell was the only candidate who promised Law and Order and the media and the public applauded him for it. The other candidates promised to fix pollution and other problems too numerous to name and were found wanting.

The primaries down the East Coast and through the South and Midwest sorted out the candidates like sand through a strainer. By the time the California primary came, there were only two left in each party vying for the job. The Democratic National Convention nominated Mitchell as their standard bearer and John Russell won the nomination for the Republicans.

During the national campaign, Casey put his support behind John Russell. Casey has great insight into Mitchell and opposed him fervently.

Once Casey contacted the Nevada Republican Committee and expressed his interest in running against Senator Clifford Wilson, they embraced him with every ounce of joy they could muster. Casey warned them that he was not the best speech maker around and he suffered from stage fright, but he would be happy to talk to the people on their home turf.

Casey only had to campaign in the cities and towns in Nevada, not the whole country. Bruce and Chuck and their campaign organization set up tours of the state to every little city they could. He talked to committeemen personally, he attended meetings and forums in Reno, Carson City, Virginia City, Las Vegas, Wendover, Elko, Riviera, McDermitt, Sparks and Owyhee.

Even though Casey doesn't make speeches well, he meets people well and they loved him. He traveled around the state three times during the campaign and met everyone he possibly could. Possibly the biggest boost to his campaign was when Governor Fairhope immediately published a letter endorsing Casey for the seat, even though they were members of opposing parties.

The November election told the tale. Mitchell was elected President by the narrowest of margins ever recorded. Mitchell and his First Lady, Annika addressed the press with his acceptance speech shortly after midnight of election day even though the count was not complete. Casey on the other hand won handily over the incumbent Senator from Nevada. Casey only failed to carry the precincts surrounding Las Vegas.

"Listen guys, we may have won this election, but we aren't any closer to solving the riddle of how to get back to where we want to be and find my Teresa."

"That's it! You just gave me the answer!" Coolie said. "We have to go to the dome and work it out. Chuck, you stay with Casey as a liaison and I'll call you when we have it ready. Let's go."

Inaugural Address
Jan 20, 2040

Most of Mitchell's speeches were received with indifference and unconcern. This one, however, was applauded by all, citizens and media alike. Prison reform has been too long in coming and Law and Order was the key that won the election for Mitchell.

"For years the Federal and State Correctional Facilities have been a place of milk and honey for the inmates who resided there. Our prisons should not be rest homes or country clubs for criminals."

"Our prisons should be terrible places where children are afraid to go. They should be places where no one would ever want to go, and they will be. If a criminal is sent to prison then that criminal should expect to pay the price for his deeds, or misdeeds."

"We must embrace Law and Order and eliminate the criminals and law breakers from our society, no matter to what lengths it takes us. They are they rats living in the filth of society and I will hire a cleaning crew to clean up the filth and exterminate the rats from where we live."

"It is time that we have lower taxes and higher employment here at home. Once the rats are eliminated, the drain on our economy will cease for this kind of problem and we will have the funds to provide more and better highways, more jobs and better living conditions for all." Mitchell said.

Prison Reform
Feb. 1, 2040

Mitchell Cordel was inaugurated President of the United States eleven days ago. Today he announced a new Prison Reform Program in a speech from the oval office. The American Public have no idea what his Prison Reform package contains, but they seemed to approve it in the polls taken prior to the election.

The following Monday, each and every prisoner who was sitting on death row in every Federal Prison across the country was executed. This event went without any fanfare or attention at all by the self-righteous press.

Monday was execution day, Tuesday was burial day and Wednesday was moving day. It is certain that the inmates of these prison systems got a real taste of fear during those last days and weeks of their lives.

Each Wednesday, those empty cells on death row were refilled from the prison population and for all intents and purposes there were prisoners on death row just as there had been the week before. As before, all of the prisoners sitting on death row in prisons across the country were executed, again on Monday.

This procedure was followed to the letter in all Federal Correctional Facilities during the months of February, March and April 2040. Some of the smaller facilities took less time to execute all of the inmates of that prison, but soon all of the Federal Prisons were empty.

A few reporters of the print and television media got a tip through a leak and reporters with cameras and microphones showed up at prisons throughout the country. But to no avail.

Reporters and cameramen were banned from entering any Federal Correctional Facility for any reason. In one instance, guards were called to break up a skirmish with reporters and guards at the gate of one facility. The reporters still did not enter.

Soon the Correctional Facilities located in the states across the country followed the pattern laid out. This, of course, set the media in motion, making all sorts of sensational charges. Had they only known the truth.

Once the public finally heard what was happening they cheered. However, the media demanded in every newspaper, television and radio news broadcast that the public rise up in arms against the government and the President for such terrible criminal behavior.

"He should be fired!" One national news anchor charged.

Impeachment talks skittered around through the press, but nothing was done.

"He should be made to resign!" Another talk show host chided.

A third, on his Saturday night telecast, said he was inhuman and should be executed along with the prisoners. Funny, this big talking newsman failed to report to work on Monday and he wasn't available for comment and we haven't seen him on that news show since then.

However, each and every member of the public, when interviewed by these same media reporters, all had similar reactions to the reporters questions.

"All those prisoners were in prisons because they had perpetrated crimes, most of which deserved the death penalty and we applaud it. Keep up the good work."

As with the Federal Correctional system, the States decided that Monday would be execution day, and Tuesday was burial day, the inmates carried the bodies out of the prison, dug the graves and completed the burial. Wednesday was moving day, once the death row cells were emptied, they were refilled by the next available inmates.

Soon all the State prisons were emptied as well and prisoners began to be moved from the smaller facilities to the larger. Soon mental institutions housing the criminally insane and other unruly patients were also bussing them to the nearest state facility for execution. County jails were also contributing busloads of unruly prisoners to the now empty State correctional facilities.

By the Fourth of July 2040, every Federal and State prison in the country was completely empty.

Mental Hospitals and Institutions were housing bona fide mental patients, county jails contained only drunks and small time lowlifes and city jails were also nearly empty with the exception of those guilty of being drunk and other such misdemeanors. But the populace did learn a valuable lesson from Mitchell. If you go to jail, there is a very good chance you will never come out.

Mitchell had an Executive Order written to close all State Prisons with the exception of one per state and later next year, these vacant prisons will be used as Government University Facilities. The Universities will teach government thinking which is presently being espoused by the President of the United States, Mitchell Cordel.

One prison in each state will remain a prison and one jail in each city will remain a jail. All others will become Government Institutions of Higher Learning.

Mitchell also slipped another little gem in with his Prison Reform package that no one noticed. According to paragraph sixteen, it is against Federal law to speak any language other that English. If you are caught it will mean jail time, and therefore, according to the Prison Reform Act, execution.

During the early weeks and months of his administration, Mitchell appointed many people to Cabinet posts and positions of importance throughout the government. A new post which he created, was the Secretary of Enforcement, to which he appointed Bobby Nash.

Of course, Bobby has a wealth of experience in enforcement as the Imperial Wizard. The Prison Reform Act and the operation and security of all the Federal Prisons were placed under Bobby. The new Chief of Staff is Jolly Rodgers.

Mitchell liked Executive Orders, and once the Prison Reform was complete, he wrote one declaring him a new term of ten years, instead of the traditional four year term.

"I didn't think being President would be this much fun"

Indian Purification
June 1, 2040

The newly elected American President Mitchell Cordel instituted the Indian Purification Program on June 1, 2040 to remove unwanted species from the United States population base. His troops hunted all the Indians down like animals and purified them as quickly as possible.

Sometime in October, word was passed along the chain of command to Jolly and then to Mitchell that the last of the Indians had been purified. This fact became the main point of discussion in the White House conference room with Mitchell and his cabinet members.

"Now that all the Indians are gone, the Blacks should be scheduled to be purified soon."

"When?"

"We'll start on Martin Luther King Day next year." Mitchell said.

Raucous laughter broke out in the meeting and Mitchell had to call a halt to the meeting until a semblance of order could be restored.

Black Purification
Martin Luther King Day
January 21, 2041

Mitchell's plan for the purification of all black people in the United States was simple. He would encourage all the blacks in the country to come out and march to celebrate Martin Luther King Day. Mitchell assigned Bobby and his men to the Black Purification Project. It would take place at every park and parade ground available.

Bobby and his staff were tasked to arrange special events, parades, anything to bring crowds together so they could be purified. During which time, Bobby's troops will move into position and use the cameras on the largest groups and eliminate any that remain by whatever means is necessary,

"Time is critical. Everyone must act at exactly the same time so there will be no notification given to warn others. Those of you in Eastern Time will fire at two p.m., Central Time, one p.m., Mountain Time, noon and Pacific Time at eleven am. Set your watches as soon as you are in your city." Bobby said.

"You're in charge of enforcement it's your job." Mitchell said.

"It's all taken care of. I have men traveling to every major city in the country for this operation." Bobby said.

"I want this done by April."

"Why."

"We will start on the Hispanic Purification Program on the Fifth of May, which is called Cinco de Mayo. You will direct the same program at that time and be completely finished before the Fourth of July. I don't want our Independence Day celebration ruined." Mitchell said.

Each two enforcement troops were instructed to go around their city with their camera and purify all who they came in contact with. A pair were sent to every large city in the country, one cameraman and one assistant to carry the "Film" pack. Each pair was given strict instructions to call in to the headquarters when they were in place.

Simultaneously across the country, the same scripted words were heard in parks in every time zone.

"Attention ladies and gentlemen, the local newspaper wants to publish a photo of today's festivities, please assemble for a photo."

FLASH!

Hispanic Purification
May 5, 2041

The plan for the purification of all Hispanic People in the United States was a carbon copy of the one which was so successfully implemented only five short months ago.

He would encourage all the people with a Spanish speaking heritage in the country to come out and march to celebrate Cinco de Mayo. As before, Mitchell assigned Bobby and his men to the Project, and as before, it would take place at every park and parade ground available.

Bobby and his staff were tasked to arrange special events, parades, anything to bring crowds together so they could be purified.

The second time, the arrangements were much easier and less time consuming. Bobby's troops will move into position and use the cameras on the largest groups and eliminate any that remain by whatever means is necessary.

Simultaneously across the country, the same scripted words were heard in parks in every time zone.

"Attention ladies and gentlemen, the local newspaper wants to publish a photo of today's festivities, please assemble for a photo."

FLASH!

Mitchell was feeling very good about himself.

"We did it! I finally did it! I told them I'd get them for what they did to me. And I did!"

"What now boss?"

"There are two things I think we should do. First I have declared myself Praefectus Pro Vita, or PPV, which means President for Life.

Second I think we should invite more Europeans to our shores. Let's have a summit with the Prime

Minister of England to tell him we welcome immigration from their country.

Another of Mitchell's Executive Orders said, "No photos may be taken of the President or any cabinet member or other government person without prior written permission from the Secretary of Enforcement. Permission will be for that event only, and failure to get permission will be punishable by a jail sentence."

As most people already know, any person sentenced to prison will go to the one remaining Federal or State facility nearest to the offender and be executed on the following Monday.

Summit Meeting, London, England
March 2041

"Joanne, my wife would like to visit her grandparents when we make the Europe trip. We will visit King Arvid of Sweden first and return to pick her up after the visits to King Gregor of Norway, King Hendrik of Denmark and the Prime Minister of England, Edward Fitzhugh."

"Yes Mr. President, I will make all the arrangements."

The visits to the four countries were of one theme, immigration. Mitchell told all four that he wished there were more of their countrymen coming to America and there was no restrictions on their emmigrating to America.

During the England leg of the journey, the paparazzi swarmed all over the American President and took photos of every little thing.

Because Mitchell and Delmer made the weapon to look like a camera, all cameras and equipment were inspected prior to any press conference or other media event.

Permission for the carrying and use of any cameras will be for that event only. The permission will not follow the reporter or photographer. But these rules did not apply in foreign countries, and these people must be dealt with in other ways.

"Bobby, get rid of these obnoxious photographers. They are disturbing all of us." Mitchell said.

"All right, you've had your fun, now beat it. All of you." Bobby said.

"What are you going to do to us? You can't stop us. We have a right to be here." One reporter said and laughed.

Bobby motions to a pair of his trusted troops to bring their camera around to an advantageous place to take a picture.

"We're only going to take your pictures. Go ahead guys."

FLASH!

"The United Nations and their one world government, that's a laugh! We are the one world government! I have a Swiss bank account with over a hundred million in it and four of the most luxurious mansions in the Caribbean islands. If that's not good government, I don't know what is." Mitchell said.

Chapter 16
Correcting Faults

November 2041

"We all know that the source of the global aggravation is the comet. We have established that the particles came from the comet and that the comet should not have approached earth, therefore we know that we must destroy that comet in order to get back to where we should be." Coolie said.

"How do we stop the comet? That is past tense."

"Exactly the answer, past tense. We must fly back in time and space to the time that the comet was approaching the earth and stop it in its tracks."

"We'll need some firepower and some way to carry the payload to the comet." Ken said.

"We will need to calculate light years and go back in time based on that calculation. We will also need to calculate the force need to destroy or deflect the comet." Bruce said.

"A small one place spaceplane was designed and built by NASA prior to the huge transports. This original design was used to test and prove the uses of Roamer and Spector. It is in good working order and is strong enough to do the job. We will install weapons for this purpose. It is in a hangar far at the rear of the secured area, waiting on us." Chuck said.

"Then what are we waiting for?"

The team went to work on the preparations for the little plane with a vengeance. It would take more than three months to install and test the systems to make the small plane ready.

Three pair of rocket powered bombs were added, along with sensors and a new larger video screen. Roamer, Spector, an autopilot system, the on-board computer with Auto Return have already been installed.

Now that Casey won the Senate seat, he is traveling to Washington more and more, but he hasn't come up with a way to stop Mitchell and it is eating him up inside.

"Senator, a man named Fred is on the phone for you."

"Yes Fred, how can I help you?"

"I think we have the answer. You must come to Nellis immediately."

Finally! This was the call he had waited for more than ten years.

"Lois, I must go to Nevada on urgent business. Someone will contact you when I return."

He couldn't get out of there fast enough.

"Computer, recognize Casey MacKenzie."

A young familiar female voice answered. It was like he was out on a drive with Chuck, and Yvonne was doing the talking.

"Good morning, Commander. How may I help you?"

"All systems on." Casey said.

"Systems on."

"Secure all openings and prepare for flight."

"Ready."

"Begin takeoff roll."

The little plane began to move forward down the runway.

"Show our present position and heading on main screen."

The main screen lit with a small plane shaped icon on a dotted line around representation of the Earth.

"Engage Roamer and proceed to point A. Execute."

The main screen presentation changed to the plane icon.

"Computer."

"Yes sir."

"Set course, time and date of contact, AR and memory modules."

"Yes sir, time set, Auto Return set, engaging memory module, to play into speaker."

"Course laid in."

"Execute."

"Energize Spector and set time to 1926, engage Auto Return and proceed to point B."

"Yes sir, time set, Auto Return set, engaging memory module to play into main speaker."

"Execute."

Through the front window, Casey saw the comet moving along its course past Neptune as the memory module gave Casey the details.

They all knew that the weapon was too small for the job and it would take a lot of luck to accomplish this task. The comet was rotating very slowly when it came into Casey's view.

Casey fired when he reached the preset coordinates which were to be the exact designated range from the comet. Both rocket powered bombs hit the comet and exploded exactly as designed, but the comet moved only imperceptibly. However the speed of rotation increased minutely as recorded by the sensors.

Casey fired again, two more rocket powered bombs reached their target with the same effect as before. Casey fired the last two, which hit again in nearly the same spot as before, but with the same effect.

The sensors recorded only the tiniest of movement of the comet, but he was now unarmed and there was only one thing to do. He returned to the predetermined Auto Return point.

"Computer standby with Auto Return sequence."

"Standing by."

"Execute."

Casey landed the little plane on the runway and taxied to the hangar which was specially outfitted for the plane. Chuck, Bruce and the rest of the team were waiting in the hangar. Casey noticed that the sky seemed a little bluer and the air felt a little cleaner.

"I'm sorry, I gave it everything I had, but it didn't move more than a hair on my sensors. As soon as we can reload and refuel I'll try it again."

"Casey, don't worry about it. Let's go inside the dome and sit for a minute."

Casey walked into the lounge and sat with the guys.

"Come on, are you going to tell me what happened to the comet? Am I the only one who knows what's going on around here?" Casey said.

In their rush to accomplish this most important task, the team forgot to wear their memory modules. The equipment was laying on the coffee table in the lounge area. Casey picked them up and gave one to each man. After the recordings played, they all seemed to come back from outer space and began to talk with Casey about the recent trip.

On another table was a small paperback book entitled "Comets of the Twentieth Century". Casey picked it up and began to page through it aimlessly.

Coolie broke the silence.

"I put that book there so you could see how well you did with the comet. Our comet was named Shoemaker-Levy 9, and was discovered on the night of March 24 1993. The discoverers thought it had been in a rapidly changing orbit around Jupiter for several decades."

"The comet was captured by the Jovian gravitational pull and during a very close turn near the planet, the unequal gravitational attractions broke the comet apart into more than twenty fragments.

The comet began to fragment during this closest approach to Jupiter and all of the large fragments were strung out in a nearly straight line pointed at Jupiter. It became known as 'the string of pearls'."

"The disruption of a comet into multiple fragments is an unusual event, the capture of a comet into an orbit about Jupiter is even more unusual, the collision of a large comet with a planet is an extraordinary event."

"Twenty one fragments were observed to impact the planet at a speed of 60 km/sec. They collided with Jupiter on July 16 to 22 1994. Jupiter is the largest of the planets and it absorbed it with no apparent injury. There are 20 pages devoted to this celestial body in this book."

"In short, you did it!" Coolie said.

They all cheered for Casey and shook his hand and patted him on the back.

"Now that your first task is complete, you must finish the second. There is no way around it, you must remove him from the timeline."

"Remove?"

"Yes. Cordel must be eliminated from both timelines. You must terminate him."

"I think I have the perfect place to do the job." Casey said. "Let's get this finished."

Casey gave them the exact time and place for the event he had in mind and they adjusted the controls and recorded the new memory module tape for all of them.

FLASH!

Casey found himself standing in a room with a chalkboard hanging on the wall and many chairs and tables in the room. The memory module told him where he was and what his mission was. He looked at the clock on the wall and knew he had to hurry to be in his appointed place.

SMHS won their first game to put them into the quarter finals, but then they came up against the toughest team they had ever faced and lost twenty one to seven. This devastating loss put them out of the running for the state title.

"It was your fault we lost that game, we should be State Champs." Mitchell was yelling at Casey again. Something he had been doing for twelve years now. "I'll get you for this!" Casey had heard it all before.

About once each year every year since the beginning of school, Mitchell tried to beat up Casey in a fight and their senior year was no exception. Connecting the school with the new gymnasium was a long enclosed hallway with three steps to the lower level that was the last bit of concrete poured before the contract was finished.

Later that week Mitchell was hiding in wait at the far end of the hall for Casey and ran down the long hall trying to catch Casey off guard as he entered the gym. Casey has studied with Mr. Soo for ten years now and a little thing like a charging rhino could not beat him.

Casey was standing in the janitors closet there in the hall way as Mitchell charged toward the gym. Carefully, Casey tipped over a bucket of water which was next to the door, just before Mitchell ran past the janitors closet.

The blindly charging Mitchell slipped on the wet cement floor and his feet flew high into the air and he fell down the steps, landing on his head.

Casey heard a loud crack and saw young Mitchell go limp at the bottom of the steps. Casey stayed in the closet until his friends ran out of the gym and found Mitchell, and the kids ran to Mitchell laying there in the hall.

"How is he?"

One of the girls who had been saying that she wanted to be a nurse pushed in beside him and put her hand on his jugular vein.

"He's dead."

They all screamed and ran for help and Casey pressed the Auto Return switch in his pocket.

Casey returned to the same spot inside the dome where he was when he left, but the dome is dark with artificial light and not the same buildings are to be seen. He walked around until someone saw him and recognized him.

A pretty young woman asked him, "May I help you, sir?"

"I seem to have got turned around, I don't recognize anything."

"Come with me, sir."

He followed her to an office door.

"I think this is the office you are looking for."

"Thank you miss, what was your name?"

"Paula, sir, Paula Rivera."

Chuck was sitting behind the desk in the office as Casey entered. Chuck was wearing a memory module and as Casey walked in he removed it and stood up to greet his old friend.

"How long have you been here?" Chuck asked.

"Ten minutes, no more." Casey said.

"Your trip was very successful, as you can see."

"See what? I have never seen any of this before."

"Walk with me I'll fill you in."

Chuck and Casey walked out of his office and down a hall toward the room occupied by the lab in the other dome.

"Let's step in here, it's quiet and no one will hear us."

"Your trips were both big successes. The comet was deflected enough to be captured by the gravitational pull of Jupiter and destroyed. After that the air and other pollution gradually began to clear.

The biggest success was the elimination of Mitchell. We knew where you were and what you were doing, because the second that Mitchell died, the two timelines folded together and here we are."

"Here we are where? Where are we?"

"In the dome." Chuck said.

"But it's dark there." Casey said pointing to the upper parts of the dome. "My watch says ten after ten in the morning and its dark. If this were the dome, I could see light." Casey said.

"Oh that, the dome is in a different place in this time. We are in Badwater Basin."

"Sorry, I don't know where that is."

"You remember Lake Mojave, don't you?" Chuck asked.

"You know I do, we were on the phone when it happened."

"You are standing in the deepest part of the lake right now." Chuck said.

"Now let me explain as much of the other stuff to you as I can. Mitchell had everyone he didn't like purified with the stolen Spectors. Most of them are here, on this side, he only sent them across like you did that time."

"A few of them didn't survive the transition, but not many. All the people who left earth for Olympus are gone and we hope they are surviving and building a new civilization there very well. When the two planes exploded in the hangar that day, we lost all connection with them."

"There will be some surprises for you. We were gone for many years and much happened on this side. Come on, let's look around this place." Chuck said.

Chuck took Casey around the new dome and pointed out many new things to him. A young smartly dressed man hurried up to them.

"Excuse me, sir, but your wife called, she wanted to know if you're going to work all night or come home to dinner, and would you pick up your daughter from band practice on the way home."

"Tease? Called? Here?"

"This daughter, she wouldn't be six years old would she?"

"Why yes, sir, but she's your daughter you should know better than I." He said.

"You didn't happen to hear her name."

"Susan." Chuck said quietly.

"Thanks. Talk about surprises."

"It's time for you to go home to your wife and kids, let's get back." Chuck said.

As they were walking back to Chuck's office, Chuck motioned to an Air Force Officer to come to them. The officer saluted as he approached them.

"This is Captain Hicks, he will be your driver. He will take you home and pick you up Monday."

Casey followed Captain Hicks down the escalator into the tunnel, along the moving floor to the elevator and up to the helicopter hangar. They boarded the helo and taxied out onto the takeoff circle. It was a short enjoyable flight to the airport.

"Hey, this is Carson City!" Casey said.

"Yes sir, it is. There is our car." The Captain said pointing to the black car waiting near the hangar.

Casey and the Captain disembarked and found their seats in the car and they were off again. The car stopped in front of a red brick building where two men dressed in dark suits were standing with a young girl of about six years. When the car came to a stop, one of the men opened the door and the little girl ran into the car and jumped onto Casey's lap.

"Daddy!"

She hugged him so hard he was surprised. The man closed the door and Captain Hicks drove on. The little girl hugged and talked a mile a minute all the way until the car stopped in front of the house on Paloverde Street.

When the car stopped this time he saw Teresa and the boys standing on the front porch. Susan alighted first and ran to her mother and hugged her, but Teresa was far more interested in the other passenger in this car. She hugged and kissed Casey until Captain Hicks cleared his throat to speak.

"See you Monday, Mr. President." He said as he entered the car to leave.

THE END

AUTHOR BIOGRAPHY

D. J. McAllister was born in St Francis Hospital in Colorado Springs, Colorado.

As a child, he bought and carried small arms and rifles into the Rocky Mountains of Colorado near his home.

He is six feet tall and weighs 188 pounds with dark brown hair, hazel eyes and glasses.

He spent two years as a member of the US Army Signal Corps, where he learned skills of an electronics technician.

After his discharge from the army, he attended the University of Colorado and earned an Associate Degree in Electrical Engineering, he also holds an FCC 1st Class Radiotelephone License.

For a brief period, he worked as an entry level engineer at a local Colorado Springs radio station.

For the next three years, he worked as a technician in the Communications and Electronics shop as Radio Repairer at Fort Carson, Colorado.

He completed his BA in Business at Wichita State University by going to classes nights and weekends while holding a full-time job.

He lived for several years in Wichita, Kansas and Kansas City and has traveled to many other places across the country. He has written many of his and his friend's unusual experiences over the years.

His Dad, Charles, retired as a CW4 after 20 years. He worked for the Santa Fe Railroad until he died. He has one brother, Sean and one sister, Doreen.